TALES TO GIVE YOU NIGHTMARES

A short story collection

By

D P Sloan

D P Sloan made you feel as though you were being followed in Go To Sleep part one. Being hunted in Go To Sleep part 2. Now settle down in your bed and read the stuff of nightmares that have plagued him for such a long time.

Witness the demons that drove him to write the horror unleashed on his fans.

Feel the tension as he shows you the dark side.

Welcome D P Sloan's Tales To Give You Nightmares.

Just don't read before you……..GO TO SLEEP!

Authors Note

I wanted to create a short story collection since I was sixteen and had my first truly scary nightmare. In this book you will find short stories that truly scared me and now I share them with you.

ABOUT THE AUTHOR

D P Sloan was born in Drumchapel, Glasgow, in 1980. From an early age like the majority of 1980's kids, he became hooked on horror movies.
It was the publication of his first novel *Go To Sleep* that set him on his way to his present position.
Go To Sleep was followed closely by the sequel Go To Sleep 2. He lives in Dalmuir, Clydebank, with his wife Rachael and their children Rebecca and Ryan and their beloved cats Honey, Freddy and Tucky.

You can follow D P Sloan on Facebook at
www.facebook.com/GoToSleepseries

For my children, Rebecca & Ryan - Daddy loves you.

For my beautiful wife Rachael - words cannot describe how much you mean to me.

For my entire family, thank you for believing in me and listening and reading my stories which are sometimes horrific.

Based on nightmares by the author

ALSO BY D P SLOAN

GO TO SLEEP
GO TO SLEEP 2

THE CLYDE

Father please forgive me for I know not what I do. I just never had the chance to ever meet you. Therefore I did not know what I would grow up to be. My mother's evil seed and do these evil deeds. That's right my mother gave birth to me - the evil one, the dark soul. I in turn began my journey to the dark-side. A journey I wanted to take, a journey to sick and deprived that you will journey with me.

Are you ready?

It was a cold May morning, Friday the 29th to be precise. I didn't go to work that day as I had, 'other plans,' those plans were to, 'get rid,' of the decomposing body rotting in the boot of my car. The best place to get rid of this kill was to, 'toss,' it in the river Clyde. A river man-made that things, 'get lost,' all the time in. It was 3am and the coast was clear. I stood on the banks of the Clyde, just west of Old Kilpatrick. The body lay in my car boot. I checked the area again, but I was safe. I retrieved my package from my car and heaved it up over my shoulder, (surprisingly the body didn't feel all that heavy.) I walked over to the banks and tossed the body down in front of me. The old carpet I used to hide the body in done well for me. I know you're wondering - fingerprints, DNA, but that my friend was all taking care of.

Rule number 1: always wear latex gloves.

Rule number 2 always wear some sort of rain coat (PVC or plastic is ideal)

Rule number 3 wear a hat of some sort.

Rule number 4 never ever use anything from your house.

The carpet came from a dumpsite - perfect. I kicked the body making it roll down the embankment and that's when I heard it - a muffled moan - a cry for help.

Then the carpet moved!

My bloody victim was still alive!

I raced down the embankment, pulled out my knife and cut the twine holding the carpet together. My victim stared up at me, don't worry he couldn't get up or scream for help. You see early, I cut off both of his legs at the knees and feed them to my very hungry dog and my tank of piranhas. I then put duct tape over his mouth and wrapped some around his arms. I swear to god when he stopped breathing I thought, 'yes at last.' Oh how wrong I was.

I looked him directly in the eyes and said, "You are going for a swim now, well in fact you won't be, you'll be building sandcastles at the bottom of the Clyde."

I raised the knife and plunged it deep into his chest causing blood to flow thick and fast. He took his last gasp and died there and then. All I did next was roll the body into the river and watch it sink.

Now take note people when a homeless tramp asks you for, '50 pence for a cup of tea.' This is how you handle the crisis.

MY SUBJECT

Have you ever been hated or discriminated against. I have that's why I did this. I've always wondered how much pain I could cause someone who hated me. Always wondered how much pain a human body can withstand before giving up for good. This hater of mine was my subject, my experiment. Let's just see how much hate I can spill from his crap infested body.

You are about to go on a journey far darker than your holiday to Spain would be. A journey direct to hell where you'll witness first hand, how to succumb and overturn any hater that bitches behind your back. Talks trash about you.

The bully at school, your workmate or even a member of your family. I had him nailed to a chair (nailed I hear you say) yes nailed like our lord Jesus Christ was nailed to the cross, I had hammered nails into has hands into the arms of the chair. Had hammered nails through his feet right into the floor. (No chance of moving now jackass are you?)

"You arsehole," he yelled at me through gritted teeth.

"Sticks and stones," I cackled back at him, "for years you have pissed me off. It was only sooner rather than later, that my dark-side would have come back."

I picked up my serrated knife and swiped it across his cheek. Blood poured from the 2 inch deep gash. I smiled as he writhed in pain.

"You fucking arsehole, when I get out of here. I'm going to kill you!" he screamed.

I smirked, "Really? You're going to kill me? Really? Listen you little piece of shit. I'm not the one nailed to a chair, am I?"

"Let me loose, let's see who is tough!" he yelled.

I grabbed my Stanley blade and swiped it across his forehead. Blood seeped down into his eyes.

I smirked again, "You won't survive to kill me!"

He wriggled about, but every time he moved, his hands and feet ripped even more.

He yelped in pain.

"So tell me," I began, "Do you want to tell me something? You know tell me to my face?"

He looked confused, "I don't know what you're talking about!"

So once again I swiped the blade across his face in a way it looked like he had a, 'Chelsea smile.'

He screamed this time and as he screamed, his cheeks opened up in one big smile.

"I love the way you lie," I told him, "you know I hate two-faced people. And I thought this was the best way to solve our little……problem."

"Please…..please stop," he blubbered, tears mixing with his blood.

I leaned into him, "I'm not going to stop until you tell the truth!"

"Ple-," he started. But I finished it for him with another swipe with my serrated knife. This time across his bare upper body. From groin to sterna. It was a deep gash, deep enough to see the fatty deposit below the skin.

I loved it!

He screamed and screamed a little bit more. Blood oozed from all cuts I inflicted on him.

"Please just stop!" He spat out.

So I did. I stopped the cutting, placing the knife back on the tray and……picked up a metal pole and turned to face my victim.

"Now you want to tell me anything to my face?" I asked rolling the pole in my hands.

No answer from him. Just more painful yelps.

"So I take it, you are scared then?" I asked.

No reply.

So I raised the metal pole and cracked him, once, twice, three times across the head and then for the finale I rammed the metal pole deep into his chest, ripping through the front of the body through to the back. I pulled the pole out, leaving a nicely formed blood and flesh dripping hole.

He gurgled his last gasp of air.

He was dead.

I smiled, I sigh of relief. It was over, I didn't get my answers. But I was satisfied. As I looked on at my victim I knew I wasn't finished yet. I dropped the metal pole, went over to his now dead body. Reached into the gaping hole and pulled (forcefully) out his still beating heart.

I looked at it and smiled, "Have a heart brother!"

WE ARE WHAT WE EAT

So there I was standing over them, a whole family lay on the floor, blood pools around them all.

Oh the joys I jumped up and down (I felt like a kid in a sweet shop!) I knelt down next to the father of the family and placed my hand deep inside the gaping hole I made in his chest, I scooped out his heart (have you ever held a human heart while it was still ...hot?) I starred at it then bit into it, emmmmmm the taste of human flesh, raw meat, you know that saying, 'it tastes like chicken!?!' Well it does although tougher than chicken - just a bit though!

I wiped the blood away from my mouth. Next was the mother, I was thinking maybe I should try her intestines. So I carved into her stomach and placed my hand deep inside pulling (or as it was hard) yanking at them. After a few seconds out came the intestines, (with a soft, 'pop,' noise. I looked at them - it was a string of sausage links! So I tried them, and may I say it was very tough to bite into them! And they tasted rather salty but hey I was hungry so it'll do.

Next was the dessert and what better way to end off a lovely meal with a bowl of fried brains in gravy. Ok so it's not ice cream but this is my meal not yours. I bent down over the lovely beautiful nineteen year old daughter of the family, took my Stanley blade (what you thought I had a scalpel?) For Christ's sake I'm a cannibal not a frigging surgeon!

I started to cut around her hairline and pulled back the scalp up over and away from her skull. I then took the claw-hammer (which I used to bash her over the head with) well she would have to be the first person to open the door to me. I began cracking the skull open with the hammer (it was like cracking a coconut open!) Then I saw the grey matter, the essence of life, the machine behind the human body - the brain. I cut the membrane open (that's the sack keeping your tiny brain in so it doesn't bounce about!) With my blade and there was my dessert, so I delved in with both hands and pulled at the young brain. It just popped out but as it was attached to the brainstem I had to cut it away, I thought that was it, time for me to fry it, but there dangling from it was the eyes.
Yuck!

I don't want the eyes! (Please note, eyes taste awful - never ever eat the eyes, the way they pop in your mouth!)

So off they came with one swipe of my blade. I began cutting a few slices of the brain, and scooped them up, went to the kitchen, booted up the cooker and grabbed the frying pan, a little oil and popped the slices of brain into pan. I watched as it fried away nicely. After a few minutes it was ready, the gravy was thick and ready too. I placed the brain in the bowl covered it in gravy and moved towards the table. I sat down and began slicing into it. It tasted so good, but I got interrupted as I neared the end of my three course meal.

Cause bang! In comes these cops through the door all pointing guns at me!

What did I do wrong?
I'll tell you shall I?
I murdered my family.

I SEE HIM

Is there anybody out there? It feels like I'm talking to myself. Can anyone hear me; I guess I keep crying to myself.

I kept running, running away from the shadow, that's what I came to call it. I thought it was a figment of my imagination. Something that wasn't really there, but low and behold there it was it followed me everywhere, reflecting off metal. I could see it, and it could see me. It always glared at me with those dark eyes. Eyes I called, 'the devils eyes.' But it wasn't the devil that I was sure of. The devil is nothing like this - this thing.

I kept running and running but no matter where I ran to, it was there, watching, waiting, waiting for me, and waiting to take me.

"Run, run little man, run away fast," I heard it snarl.

"Go away, annoy someone else - please!" I yelled back.

It laughed with such evil in the voice, "You don't know who I am, do you?"

I shook my head, "No please just leave me alone!"

It smiled back at me, looking directly in my eyes, "I'm you!"

At that point I raised my fist and smashed the mirror, and it vanished.

THE FIRST TIME

I killed him. It was my first time. First kill. And oh how it felt good!

After years of pent up frustration. Years of, 'oh I'm better because I said so!' It was time to finally release my anger. All I needn't was a sign. A sign to tell me, 'now is the time!'

And low and behold a sign was delivered. Good old water company had switched off his water. And he asked me, "Can I have a bath in yours?"

I smiled, "Anything for you."

He came round that night for his bath. What he didn't know was I broke the lock off the bathroom door.

"Sorry mate there's no lock on the door it's busted, just close it over," I told him.

He nodded.

The plan had begun.

I waited until he was in the bath for about ten minutes then I made my move. I plugged in my radio into an extension cable. I then burst into the bathroom carrying the radio; he jumped up with such a fright.

"What the hell?" he screamed.

I cocked my head from side to side, then raised the radio and threw it into the bath. He scrambled to get out but the electric current kept him in the tub. Such a great sightseeing him frazzle in the power of electricity. The smell of wet burning flesh was so overpowering I vomited just a little in my mouth. The lights flickered on and off - but I wasn't done yet. I unplugged the extension cable and gradually pulled the radio out of the water. I then retrieved a large kitchen knife and with one quick swipe I sliced opened his throat; the sight of the dark red liquid poured down his chest and turned the bath water a deep red colour.

I thought, "I ought to drink the bath water that ought to be fun."
That's when my serial killer manslaughter begun.

PAY UP, DON'T THINK SO

There ain't no grave that can hold my body down.
I've tried and tried to kill myself.
I've tried drowning myself by jumping into the Clyde - that didn't work. A passing boat picked me up.
I've tried cutting my wrists - but the blade snapped.
I've tried hanging myself from the ceiling light fixture - only for the roof to cave in.
They say, death comes to those who wait. Well I've waited long enough!
You might be wondering why I'm trying to kill myself. Well I'll start at the beginning shall I?
Yesterday morning, I killed someone. You got to understand here, at first I didn't mean it. It just happened. She was there, I was there, she argued, I argued, she threw a glass at me; I threw a hammer at her. I was expecting her to duck or move out the way but no she stood there and the hammer collided with her skull.
WHACK! Then followed by a CRACK!
She fell to the ground, I looked on in horror at first but then I smiled.
"Ding dong, the bitch is dead!" I sang.
Now I had to get rid of the body.
"Cut it up," I muttered.

It had to be done. So I went into my toolbox in the cupboard, grabbed my hacksaw, my flat headed screwdriver and my Stanley blade. I returned to the body and began gouging out her eyes with my screwdriver (well what did you think I was going to use it for?) I didn't want her dead eyes staring back at me. As I gouged them out, I didn't expect the, 'POP,' noise they made as they came out of the sockets. Next was to remove her head, so hacksaw was needed. I sawed for a good 5 minutes, (it takes a lot to cut through the vertebrae.) The head came away from the body, but blood, stupid fucking blood. I wasn't expecting that.

Ok, ok I was expecting blood but not squirting out that fast.

I cut around the arm joints with my Stanley blade and also the leg joints then used my trusted hacksaw to cut through the flesh and right through the bone beneath.

The arms, legs and the head were now off. All that remained was the torso. You see I had to cut the torso too, (it was the only way it was going to all fit down the bin chute!)

I retrieved black bags, because I knew the organs would have to be put in them. Yet again I cut round the stomach area with my Stanley blade, (just to make a start,) then I used my old pal the hacksaw it cut through the thick flesh (thank god she was skinny!) I cut through the backbone and off came the lower half of the torso. Intestines and half the stomach fell to the carpet. A putrid smell came from it, I thought that has to be the stomach acid. I placed all organs into separate black bags. Then the head, arms and legs into other bags.

As it was 5pm - I started carrying out the, 'rubbish,' to the bin chute. I dropped them one at a time down the chute.

A sense of freedom came over me. I was finally free.

But today after running a blade across my wrists and it breaking. After trying to hang myself and the ceiling falling down. Then finally throwing myself into the Clyde to try and drown only for a boat to pick me up. I decided I just have to come clean and tell the council, "Listen I killed my housing officer because she demanded I pay my rent arrears now."

FAST FOOD, FAST KILL

I awoke early on Saturday the 12th of November, I starred at the clock, it read 3AM. I climbed out of bed - well what I thought was my bed, but it wasn't. I was naked in McDonalds, I don't know how I got there but I was surrounded by dead bodies.

Blood all over floor, I don't know how it got there, but I guess I must have killed them.

Just then I heard the cry, a cry of help. Although I was naked I made my way through the blood covered tiles. I made my way into the back of the fast food joint, making sure I didn't step on the severed arms and legs. Once I was in the kitchen, on my right stood the chip fryer bubbling away as if chips were in it. But it wasn't chips, it wasn't French fries - I took a closer look into the bubbling abyss and as I lifted the wire basket from the fryer - a severed head stared directly at me. I must have blacked out then because when I awoke and I was standing in Clydebank shopping Centre. This time clothed, however in my hand I held tightly a serrated knife, blood dripping neatly from it onto the tiled flooring.

Then I came too, and I heard screaming - in front of me lay a body of a teenage boy, throat cut, blood pouring all around him.

The screams came from the people looking on in horror. I looked at each and every one of them. I didn't say anything then shouting came from behind me. I turned still grasping the knife. Coming towards me was two clueless security officers and three police officers.   They started saying something but all I heard was white noise. They surrounded me but I still stood there glaring at them.

A police officer stepped forward, I took a swipe at him with my knife, only for him to grab me and force me to the ground.

I blacked out again, only to come too and stood starring at.......myself!

I watched as my body swayed gentle from side to side.

A note was attached to my trousers it read;

'I'm sorry but it had to be done. All I wanted was a plain cheeseburger. They shouldn't have made me wait!'

FACEBOOK RIPPER

You know technically I'm not even supposed to be here. But fuck it; I may as well make the most of it.

You're probably wondering what I am talking about. Well I'll tell you shall I?

Have you heard the story of the, 'Facebook Ripper?' That's me!

You still wondering what I'm talking about. Well see that wee search bar at the top of your home page. I came up with an idea that you can type in any name and up comes various people under that name.

For example let's take my subject; I typed in Carly and up came over 1000 Carly's!

9 out of 10 times, social networkers put their full name, address and phone numbers on their profile page. This makes it easy for anyone to get a hold of you. It turns out that my subject - Carly put everything on here including where she, 'checked in,' every day.

I followed my subject for weeks on end until one night she announced on her status, 'John browns pub tonight with my bestie girls for drink, drink, and more drink!'

If you are unsure of where John browns is well it's just up the road from me in Clydebank. I knew from Carly's profile, what she looked like (photos you got to love them!) Shoulder length brown hair, hazel eyes and good old St Tropez fake tan (she loved looking like a dried up prune!) Hello Carly you stay in Scotland not Turkey! She by the looks of it was a size 8 with a nice rack and a tight ass. She just blogged a pic of what she was wearing tonight.

One word bitch you look like a slut!

A tight short (very short) black dress and black high heels. (Don't see her running away fast in them from me ha-ha!)

Her profile said, 'single and want to mingle!'

So I'll play the single guy looking to hook up with a girl for some, 'wham bam thank you ma'am.'

I made sure I was visible, standing at the bar and as soon she came to get more drinks. I introduced myself,

"John," I said, "here let me get them."

She smiled, "Thanks my name is Carly." She picked the drinks up, "see you later."

I nodded, "Indeed you will."

It wasn't until later on, 1am to be precise that we all piled, I followed Carly and her, 'besties,' out the door and overheard them saying, 'Boulie time!' but dear young Carly had too much to drink and she shook her head, "No I'm heading home." The girls all hugged and said their goodbyes and off young Carly walked all on her own back home but not before noticing me, "John hi honey!" She declared.

I couldn't believe she still knew my name. I smiled back.

She came over to me, "Fancy coming back to mine?" She declared pushing up against.

She wanted me just like that, in fact if she could, we would have went behind the local kebab shop known as the, 'Nasty Spot,' and fucked each other senseless. But I didn't want my DNA on or in her.

"Yeah no problem," I replied.

We walked hand in hand. She groped me, I groped her. We walked around the back of the council offices. Nice and dark, (just the way I liked it!) As we got midway, I produced my knife (a Swiss army.) Then I grabbed her and slit her throat (ha she wasn't expected that!) She gurgled, spat up some blood, gurgled again. Then collapsed to the ground. Blood pooled around her.

"Hush little baby don't you cry," I whispered.

Now I had to make this stand out as much as Jack the ripper and bible john. So I ripped a piece of her dress and grabbed a stick lying next to her dead body. I wrapped the cloth around the stick, dipped it into the sluts blood and then I turned to the wall.
I wrote:

'I am the cleanser of these streets.'

I stood up, hid the stick far away from the scene of the kill and walked out onto the street, past the, 'Singers,' bar onto Dumbarton road, I started to cross the road not watching and……BAM!!! A BP oil tanker smacked into me rolling over my ribcage as it came to a stop just before the turning onto Kilbowie road.
I lay there on the road, not dead…….yet. I was surrounded by people that came out of the pub.
"Are you ok?" I heard someone say.
I stared up at them, "Not dead yet," I smiled.

DO YOU GIVE TO CHARITY

"Aaaaaaaaaamen, aaaaaamen, aaaaaamen, aaaaaaamen."

Feels good right?

Saying the Lord's Prayer. Gets you wondering. Does the dear Lord, our saviour (apparently) listen to us? Does he help us?

Well he doesn't help those sick and dying.

Doesn't help the homeless.

And he most certainly doesn't help me!!!!!

I prayed and prayed one night, the night I did it.

Did he listen?

Did he fuck?

There I was minding my own business, walking down Argyle Street in Glasgow; it was around 4.30pm on Saturday the 19th of November. I was in a hurry (wanted to get home for X-Factor) hey we all have our guilty pleasures. Anyway getting back to my God forsaken day (excuse the pun.) I was walking down the street and as I neared the big HMV store, I was stopped by a charity worker collecting cash for some teenage charity - help the homeless crap, (don't you just hate them!?!) hey buddy if I wanted to give to a charity, I'd give to one that doesn't get coverage - like Huntington's, PDSA, not big ones that ALWAYS get the money!

Anyway there I go again going off the path. This guy stopped me, he was wearing all black however he had a red bib over his jumper.

"Excuse me mate." He began.

First things first I ain't your mate! My mates are in far better jobs than you with your hassling shit!

I tried to get past him but he continued to follow me (like a little lost dog) well I had to stop didn't I.

"Yes what can I do for you?" I asked.

"Have you got a few minutes to spare?" he questioned.

I fucking stopped didn't I?

I didn't have a choice because you chased me down the street.

"Of course no problem," I replied.

"Thanks," he began, "would you like to donate to the teenage homeless charity. Its only £9.95 a month direct debit."

I shook my head, "No sorry I'd rather not." I began to walk away.

Then I heard him say, "Tight bastard!"

I turned to him, "What did you say?"

He looked right at me, "I'm just saying its charity."

I walked right up to him and stared him in the eyes. "Yes I am tight my friend, but I'm not a bastard. I my friend have a father."

I began to walk away again only to hear him shout, "Fuck you mister!"

That's all I needed, the streets were packed, but I turned and raced back towards him.

"Have you ever danced with the devil in the pale moonlight?" I asked.

He looked confused, "Wha-what?"

"Jack Nicholson - the Joker from the Tim Burton Batman movie - it's a saying that always stays with me when fuckers like you test me. So tell me - have you ever danced with the devil in the pale moonlight?" I told him.

He shook his head, "No."

I smiled, "Say your prayers," as I buried my knife deep into his chest cavity. His face it was a picture (where were the Japanese tourists with the cameras when you needed them!) He clutched his chest, dropping the clipboard and then stumbled back and fell over.

People started screaming - oh how sweet it sounded in the air. Kids crying, parents' running away but the ironic thing was teenagers laughed and pointed! (Oh the youth of today - you got to love them!)

I cocked my head from side to side, leaned over him and said, "I'm not a tight bastard but I am a sick bastard." I swiped my knife over his throat. Blood spurted everywhere.

I stood up put my hands out as though I was on a cross and shouted, "Jesus wept!"

I heard sirens in the distance, screams all around. People shouting, "Oh God, oh God, oh God!"

I declared to the terrified public, "I AM GOD!"

Charity begins at home first and I just proved that.

HI I'M SCHIZO, WANNA PLAY?

"I'm giving serious thought to eating your wife. I wanna play game, if you answer correctly you she will survive," that's what I told her husband the day she went missing.

I'll start at the beginning shall I?

It was 3PM on Sunday the 20th of November, I watched her from across the street. I knew she worked in the local salon, I've been watching for a long time - but she didn't know that. I've been following her home, but yet again she didn't know that. I knew she was married although she never wore a ring. I found out she was married simply by easily breaking into their house. There on the hall wall was the wedding photo of her and her dear husband.

"Let me out," she screamed, "you arsehole, let me out!" I listened to the sweet sound of her voice.

"As you can hear Dennis - your wife is scared," I cackled down the phone.

"What do you want with me?" he replied to me.

"Its simple play my game and I let her live. Don't play or lose, then I kill her and then eat her," I told him.

"Ok, ok, I'll play what's the game?" he asked.

"Name the movie that beat Freddy Vs Jason in the box office to number one?" I asked.

"Are you serious?" he began, "How the hell am I to know that?"

"Didn't you hear of Google?" I smirked, "guess you don't know then. Oh well game over already!"

"No wait, wait, WAIT!" he yelled.

But I already hung the phone up. It was time for dinner anyway.

Now where was I to start? Oh yeah I know, the brain best part of it. I turned to my darling victim with my art scalpel and began cutting around her scalp, she screamed and then went quiet. I grabbed my circular saw and began cutting the skull open. I lifted the skull cap (funny as it sounds, it does look like I just took off her hat!)

I used my scalpel again just to cut the membrane off the delectable meal in the head and then cutting into the brain itself I cut a piece off and stuck it straight into my mouth (none of this frying shit - I love my meat rare!)

I've already sought out my next victim (a high-school girl - I can't wait to taste her!)

Oh now by the way. If someone asks you a trivia question like I did to that dear husband of my dinner.

Then the answer my dear friend is:

Open Range

Ironic that isn't it?

YOU DUMMY

"Go to sleep bitch, die motherfucker die - ugh, time's up bitch, close your eyes. Go to sleep bitch, why are you still alive, how many times do I have to tell you, close your eyes so go to sleep bitch - die motherfucker die."

Oh sweet music to my ears as I piled the dirt onto her dirty naked body.

"You filthy whore," I yelled, spit flying from my mouth, "you deserve this. How dare you stare at him with your come to bed eyes!"

Another shovel of dirt over her dirty filthy body, she will curse the day she stared at him that way!

I remember the day like it was yesterday. There I was talking to her and along comes this jackass of a guy. I saw the way she twisted her head round and extended her arm to touch his cheek.

I WAS THERE FOR GODSAKES!

She ignored me so that night after work - I grabbed her while he wasn't looking, I took her to a field not far away, don't get me wrong - she didn't scream, didn't kick out - just sat there. This was going to be quick and simple.

"I loved you, and you do this to me!" I yelled. She sat there still silent. "Oh now it's the silent treatment! Listen that's fine but answer me this, do you love him?"

Still silence.

"So no answer guess that means yes then," I yelled.

I pulled the car over and pulled her out of the car. No screaming, no kicking, no punching or biting. I moved over to the already dug hole. I cracked her on the face causing her nose to cave in. She just fell back right into the hole.

Then I covered her with dirt until I couldn't see the filthy slut anymore.

I went home and slept like a baby. The next day I got up, had sugar puffs and a cup of coffee. I got my uniform on and headed to work. I walked into work smiling, happy and whistling away and that's when I saw her.

There she was standing hand in hand with him again!

How the hell can that be? I - I killed her! I buried her!

Fuck! Fuck! Fuck!

I got closer and closer and saw that she was half naked. No bra or top on and just a short skirt on.

What the hell?

I stood about 5 feet away from them and then felt the strong hand on my shoulder.

"Jeff," it was my manager, "will you stop going into your stupid dazes and do your job and dress those mannequins in the window - they are just dolls and you're a window dresser!"

BUS RIDE

I can hear your heartbeat because you're scared. I can hear your heartbeat because you're scared. See I'm a psycho, a sicko and am crazy.

I had the worst day of my life. Stood waiting for over an hour for our fantastic bus service in Glasgow should have been called second group rather than first.

Finally the number 60 turned up! (Can I have a round of applause.) I stepped onto the bus and showed my pass to the driver. He nodded and I moved into the sitting area, the bus was pretty packed so I sat next to this disgusting stinking fat slob of a man. I mean he smelled like the sewer works in Dalmuir! But I wasn't standing I couldn't, my legs you see they have been giving me bother for a while now. So there I was sitting next to this grease ball of a man. I held back the vomit cause if I didn't I was puking my breakfast up. (Why the hell did I not just stay at my dad's I mean his fiancée was making a fry-up!) If I stayed for that, I would have missed this bus with this fat-man on it and got the next one. Well if there was another bus (it is Firstbus we are talking about here people!) But just got to put up with it.

I pulled out my walker's cheese & onion crisps and opened them. I began eating them only for fat-man with his twenty chins stare at me while I ate them.

What the hell?

Pinks song played in my headphones, the fantastic, 'fucking perfect!' Bloody ironic song that when you think of the situation I was in.

"Excuse me," Mr. Blobby began, "can I have some of them?"

What the hell!

This jelly belly was asking for some of my crisps! He would probably eat his own arm off if he was starving! (Although I have to say it did resemble a chicken drumstick!)

I looked at him, "Sorry what did you say?"

"Can I have some of your crisps?" The giant marshmallow asked again.

"Eh - ok then," I answered. I moved the pack to him and he moved his greasy fingers to my packet. Then he done the worst thing - he grabbed my packet and emptied the lot into his garbage disposal of a mouth!

He licked his lips and then with a smile handed me the empty packet back to me!

"You fat bastard!" I screamed.

He just laughed causing crumbs to come spitting out at me. I stood up staring at him, I grabbed a metro newspaper off of the guy next to me, rolled it up and lunged at spare tyre man, and he looked horrified as I forced the newspaper down his throat until it was stuck. I stepped back and laughed, "Eat that you fat pie!"

He flapped about trying to get the paper out but his greasy fingers couldn't grab it.

I was pulled back and held by four big ass men. (Popeye didn't have a look in with these guys!)

The police came and then the paramedics came. They managed to get the newspaper out, but fat-man died! (Oh such a shame - not!)

The paramedics handed the police the murder weapon. The officer unrolled it and turned it to me and I laughed.

On the front page the story read:

'Government says Scottish people are overweight!'

TWO MINDS FOR THE PRICE OF ONE

She followed me constantly day in day out, not real not real, not real.
I kept on repeating it but it done me no good.
When I was at work, she was there. When I was shopping, she was there. Hell when I was at the pub having a wee drink to calm my nerves, she was bloody there!
Ok I admit it, alright I killed her, I murdered her, I murdered her - stuffed her in my freezer waited a few days then dumped her at the bowling basin. She sunk like a lead block into the quicksand like water.
Not real, not real, not real.
Then it occurred to me - it's her sister it got to be, she had to have a twin!
Not real, not real, not real.
One thing I had to do was question her on why she was following me. Yeah so I killed her (problem? I don't think so!) But she had to go. So if I tell this, this other woman this twin then I'll have a weight lifted off my shoulders!
So I waited outside the Asda store in Clydebank until I spotted her, she moved through the crowd, gliding brisk fully through the public. I moved into the massive supermarket, picked up a basket and walked up the fruit & veg aisle, and I noticed from the corner of my eye, she was following me.
Good!
I moved into the soup aisle and she followed me and that's when I turned to my female stalker.
"Why are you following me?" I questioned.
The aisle emptied fast, no sooner than normal, it was just me and her now - now time to sort this once and for all!
"So tell me why are you following me?" I asked again.
She didn't say a word; she bloody stood there just smiling!

"Ok so I killed her are you happy? I killed her and now she's sinking in Bowling Basin are you happy now?" I yelled at her.

Still no word from her, just a smile, wicked smile at that!

I lunged at her, and fell flat on my face, next thing I knew I've got six police officers on me, one saying to another, "So who we dealing with today? Jack? Jeff or the real guy David?"

I heard one cop laugh, "This guy is just cuckoo, a nutcase, and bananas literally fucking crazy!"

They hoisted me up onto my feet, "Come on David - you know you are not allowed to leave the hospital!"

They marched me out passed security and startled shoppers. They placed me in the back of the police van and closed the doors.

I heard muffled talk from outside the van, "So doc can you be certain he will stay in hospital now?"

"Of course he will. All we can do is say sorry and make sure all doors are secure in future!"

"Doc you said that last time!"

"Gartnaval hospitals got new security officers so all should be well now!"

"Ok doc, it's in your hands now."

I heard car doors closing and we set off........home.

MY EVIL SIDE

Every night I dreamt of her, my skin crawled as if I was covered in bugs. Bugs, worms feasting on my flesh. I got up every minute to puke.
Why the hell am I still dreaming of her?
Stupid woman and her idiotic boyfriend deserved to die!
But why am I just dreaming of her?
Why not him as well?
My skin itched so badly. I swear to good it was as though maggots, other bugs and worms were covering my body. I stared into the mirror of the bathroom and turned on the cold water tap. I bent down and splashed the water over my dry pale stubbled face. I stood straight up and stared into the mirror again, and there she was staring back at me. I screamed - my reflection had been replaced by her rotting corpse, I noticed a worm coming out her nose, her mouth began to open and she started to say something. But I couldn't make her out. I began to puke again, sick to my stomach. I knew I had killed them both; I cut her boyfriend's arms and legs off and disposed of them in the garbage. His head into a black bag and his torso into another bag. I bashed her over the head and constantly banged her head off the cement floor until she was dead and her head had caved in, brain matter all over the floor.
Then I buried them - in my back garden.
But now she stared back at me, her mud covered skull, her black sockets where her eyes used to reside, stared back at me.
I puked again.
What do I do now?
I left the bathroom and walked into……the garden????????
How the hell did I end up here?

I saw the disturbed earth where I buried them and then I saw it move!

Up and down, up and down. Then a hand emerged, then a head and then a torso. No, no, no the dead was rises.

Just a dream, just a dream, just a dream.

It was only just a dream.

Then the full dead corpse rose out of the earth. She stood there staring at me. Then she moved towards me. I screamed and screamed.

Then I felt the warm gloved hands of my dad holding me. I opened my eyes and watched as the order of service went without a hitch.

"Ashes to ashes, dust to dust," the priest told the group as the coffin was lowered into the ground.

"Come on Robert let's get you back to your room," my dad advised me.

I was shackled at the legs and arms and guided by my dad and the orderlies, back to the ambulance back home........to the hospital.

No one really knows what or why I killed my mum and her boyfriend that night, but I did tell them when I was arrested that the reason I did it - I thought they were zombies coming to kill me.

I now reside in this 8 by 8 room, padded with just a bed and a toilet. The doctor said I will be here for all my life.

MONEY MAKES THE WORLD GO ROUND

It was perfect, the perfect crime, and the perfect murder. Kill said person and you become rich. I enjoyed it so much and to have so much money at the end of it, just made me happier.

You obviously don't know what I'm talking about.

So I'll tell you shall I?

Debt, debt, and more debt it surrounded me everywhere I went. Hell it probably surrounds everyone reading this as I speak!

Turned down for loans upon loans, credit cards. I applied for everything and came away with nothing.

"I'm sorry Mr. Baxter but your application has been unsuccessful."

"Can I speak to the bank manager then please? I'm desperate; this recession has hit me bad!" I asked.

The assistant nodded and went to find the manager. A few seconds later a well fed man in a (very dear) Armani suit walked in. "Mr. Baxter is it," he asked extending his rich little fingers. I nodded, shaking his hand. He sat across from me and looked over the application. He shook his head. "I'm sorry Mr. Baxter; there is nothing I can do."

I put my head in my hands, "Nothing you can do. Really? Really? Nothing at all?"

"Sorry nothing at all, it's your credit rating it must be bad. You should contact either Experian or Equifax they should be able to advise you why." He smiled.

"You're smiling as though everything is ok, well it's not! I'm going to be made homeless, Brighthouse is going to take my furniture back because I've missed two maybe three payments and you smile!"

"I'm sorry!" He exclaimed.

"May I remind you, I along with every fucking taxpayer in this rip off Britain own a part of this Bank! Our tax money went to a fund to bail out this shitty bank and you turn around and say sorry! Tell me Mr. Moneybags do you still get a bonus?"

"That's nothing to do with this is it now Mr. Baxter?"

I stood up and banged my fists down on the desk, "Answer the fucking question! I've never asked for any credit such as loans off of this bank. My work cuts my hours so I can barely live. The social won't help - why? I hear you ask, simple the fucking Con-dem-nation decided to cut the social fund. So I ask you, answer my fucking question - do you still get a bonus?"

"Yes I do, every year!"

"And how much do our beloved bank managers make in a bonus every year?"

"That's irrelevant," he replied.

"Answer the fucking question!" I yelled.

"Ok - about a million, alright I'm rich; I'm happy, no worries; go home every night and drink champagne and eat extravagant meals. Is that what you want to hear?"

I smiled, "Thank you - now I'm going to ask you to push through this application for a loan and I'll leave here and everything will be fine."

"And if I don't?" He questioned.

I moved to the door and turned the lock and then closed the blinds. No one wants to see this, "Then you die. It's a simple formula, a very simple formula. We both win you see."

"Are you threatening me Mr. Baxter?" He began to stand.

"Trust me, I ain't kidding!" I unzipped my jacket pocket and produced my Swiss army knife.   His eyes went wide with shock.

"Ok, ok no need to do this!" He pleaded, hands out defending his body.

"Well fix it then!"

He turned to the pc and started typing away, "I can override every application and also give a loan to anyone without a payment due a year to the date. So, so how much?"

"Fifty grand," I asked walking around the back of him.

"That's a lot especially when your initial application was for one grand."

I put the knife to his throat, "Do it!"

He nodded, typed away again and then gulped, "That's it Mr. Baxter the money will be in your account with 15 minutes."

I looked at the PC and for once a bank manager did not lie! Then I did it, I pulled the knife across his throat, cutting a thin but perfect line. Blood poured fast.

I left the office, closed the door, walked over to customer services, told the clerk that he didn't want disturbed as he was on the phone to family. She nodded. I asked her how I make a big withdrawal. She told me I.D and bank card.

I withdrew the money and left.

Fuck recession I'm rich!

THE QUOTA

Freddy Kruger - I wouldn't piss on him if he was on fire. (Get it!?!)
Michael Myers - I would take a shit in his jack-o-lantern and tell him I'm taking over.
Jason Voorhees - I would hit him in the balls with a hockey puck and tell him its fucking on!
I am the ripper, the collector of souls and I will take yours as you have taking theirs.
Some people live a full life and then die. Some people die very young. Some people die sooner rather than later. Their souls (you think) go to heaven, some go to hell. Some stay earthbound to finish their business.
But that is all lies; I collect their souls and take them to my lord. That's my job. In some instances I must kill to fulfill my quota. In doing so people die. I'm sorry but it has to happen.
Don't think of me as the bad guy, I get, 'rid,' of the bad guys.
My latest quota had Tommy on the list. My lord wanted him personally. Apparently he wanted to torture this guy Tommy in ways that only he could.
He sent me the list on Wednesday the 23rd of November and on it, it said Thomas Mulgrew known as Tommy residing at 13 Abbotshall lane, Drumchapel. Take his life I want his soul.

Thursday the 24th November came and I set out, it had just turned 3am so the streets were dead, and it was easy to gain access to the street without being seen. Apparently street lights get turned off once in a while (to do with carbon emissions maybe I think.) I entered through the back garden, climbing over the wooden fence (sleep tight Tommy cause tonight you dine in hell) I got to the kitchen window and looked in; (all is quiet in the house. Nothing stirred not even a mouse.) I smashed the corner of the window to the door and reached in and unlocked it. The door opened (Tommy, Tommy you need to secure your house more!) I walked into the kitchen, various instruments of pain and torture lay about, (knives, meat cleavers.). I don't need any of that, I have my own toys. I walked down the hall and up the staircase. Three rooms greeted me, the bathroom and two bedrooms. I knew he was alone in his house (he only gets his daughter at the weekends.). So I bypassed his kids' bedroom and walked towards Tommy's room. I entered, and there lying sleeping like a baby was my quota for the month, the guy my lord wants for his pleasure and Tommy's pain. I walked round to the left side, unzipped my black jacket and removed my dagger, (the same dagger used to take Caesars soul) what do you think he was killed for fun? Did you think I was the only soul collector? Don't be fucking stupid! I raised the dagger high above my head - it glistened in the moonlight and then I brought it down deep into my subjects' heart. He awoke with panic but it was too late. His soul rose from his body and I pulled out my list. The soul shot straight for my list and it shone brightly as the list collected the soul.

Tommy's mere life was gone but my lord will have his soul forever.

Job done I headed home.

BULLY

November 24th was the day it started and November 25th was the day it was to end. It wasn't just 24 hours this had been going on for years; I'm not saying one day this particular thing had been on for years - seventeen years to be precise.

Are you wondering what I'm talking about well I'm talking about a bully. This bully had been annoying me since I was fourteen years old. And today I was going to, 'fix,' it. You want to know the ironic thing; my bully was now a frigging teacher!

Not only that - a teacher at my old secondary school! What are the chances of that?

I sat in my car across from the school and watched as the Drumchapel high school pupils left. I waited and waited and then he left. What's that? Ha not even in a car - he was walking! Game fucking on!

I started my car and began slowly moving towards him. He was heading down into the now demolished houses in Cally Avenue. I looked in my rear-view mirror and my side windows, good no one in sight. I parked my car, pulled up my black hood, grabbed hold of my flat headed screwdriver and hammer, climbed out the car and walked (with a good pace) towards the big bully.

As I neared him, I shouted, "Hello William." He turned round, startled by seeing me. I didn't waste time I raised the hammer and brought it (claw side) down first into his skull. It stuck! Blood spurted everywhere.

He collapsed looking up at me, "No please, no!"

I just smiled and drove the screwdriver deep into his throat ripping his carotid artery apart. I grabbed the hammer and pulled it out of his skull and then removed the screwdriver.

I smiled again, "You ain't no mother-fucking bully now!"

I turned and walked back to my car a free man.

S.T.D: SEDUCTION, TORTURE, DISMEMBER

Seduction, seduce. There isn't anybody who is as good at what I do. Because one minute she loves me, the next she don't. She's been stolen from you.

Torture, abuse. Take her by the hand and guide to the chair, show her you love right now but next you don't, it's just the way you like it.

Dismember, get rid of. Saw her in half with a chainsaw, and gut her like a fish, that's the name of the game.

Are you ready to play?

I found her propping up a bar one night, down vodka and Sambuca shots as though they were water. I managed to persuade her to come home with me. We kissed on the doorstep and as I fumbled to turn the key in the lock, she fumbled my belt buckle, trying to pull my jeans down on the doorstep. I pushed her through the front door and as we banged against each side of the hallway, stripping at the same time. I envisioned what she would see when I was ready to S.T.D her. In case you are still not clued up my S.T.D stands for:

SEDUCE, TORTURE, DISMEMBER.

Literally speaking I spread my S.T.D about this town.

I closed my eyes while I fondled her breasts, pulling her into my living room, soon I will have her skull as an ashtray and her skin as a cushion cover. But for now the seduction part.

She pulled my white t-shirt off and I pulled her skirt down, I have to say she does have a beautiful trimmed and tight body, obviously a fitness freak – me? Well I'm average, keep myself clean, a bath or shower every second day (when you live in the city, the dirt and grime just clings to your body, best to keep clean until you get covered in blood that is!)

She straddled me as we sat on my black leather couch and I entered her.

She squealed like a pig, (soon darling you will scream far worse than this!)

Up and down, up and down she bounced, her ample breasts bouncing like a space hopper.

Within (I think) 10 minutes she came (yeah I am that good.)

Stage one completed: Seduce out of the way.

She climbed off me and sat next to me, her body soaking with sweat (and other bodily fluid may I add!)

She smiled; I smiled and then whacked her over the head with my claw hammer (which was hidden next to me on the couch.) She went out like a light.

I got dressed again while she lay there nude; I burned her clothes in my coal fire. (For all you eco-friendly people out there the coal is fumeless – whatever the fuck that means!) I picked her up and put her over my shoulder, just like a fireman to the rescue. I walked down the hall, opening each room as I went.

Room 1, contained a beautiful red head girl around eighteen I dismembered her limbs and left her to bleed out.

Room 2, contained a psycho bitch, believe me she put up a good fight, (always liked a feisty bitch) but she wasn't any match for me, especially when I skewered her with a sharp piece of metal and hung her over the bath while I sliced her skin off her.

Room 3, well what can I say, this little piggy went to market and didn't come home again because she met me. She's not dead yet, but it shouldn't be to long, you see I cut her scalp off using my trusted Stanley blade. While she was awake may I add! She's in pain. Hush little girl, daddy's here no more nightmares.

I walked down the stairs into my basement-come-dungeon and placed my newest prized position on the only seat in the room, a steel chair, bolted to the concrete ground (so no falling over or escaping.)

The chair contained straps for arms and legs and the straps contained a metal ring which once secured around said victim, would then be padlocked to a chain yet again bolted to the ground.

Welcome to my nightmare.

I secured her in place and sat on the floor about 5 feet away from her, I breathed in and closed my eyes, and thought about her as though I was her.

This is what I saw:

I keep telling myself that it's all just a dream. That I'll wake up any moment now and be in my bed; that I'll eventually forget about this and move on with my day. But something keeps me from knowing that this is true. It's the pain. I've suffered too much through this for it to be a dream.

I need to get out of here. I need to find someone and escape. Oh, God, I hope he hasn't killed everyone yet. I stumble across the hallway and open every door I see. Most of the rooms are empty, but some are occupied by the corpses of his fresh victims.

Decapitation, impalement, incineration, disembowelment; you name it, he's done it. All of this, just to please his twisted desires. He needs blood. He needs torture. He needs death. Everything about it gives him a sexual high like no other. I've seen him orgasm when he tears his victims' apart limb from limb. His moans and cries of pleasure still fill my ears and make me sick to my stomach.

I start to tremble. No, not now... don't let the pain kick in now! I need to keep going. I need to find someone and get the hell out of here. Blood flows down my arm, matching the pulsations of my heart. I open another door. Damn! This one's empty too! Has he killed everyone already? Have I been walking around here for nothing?

I hear footsteps. No... no not yet! NOT YET! I need to keep going. Keep running. Open the doors.   Escape... fading... nothing... I'm not... ready to die... n-not yet...

I wake up. All there is around me is darkness. I try to move, but I'm strapped to a table. Damn! I failed! He got me and now I'm back right where I started. I can hear cries in the other room. No… he didn't kill everyone! I could have saved someone! If it hadn't been for my damn shoulder!

Tears start to form in my eyes. As they cascade down my face, I start to break down. I don't want to die. I don't want to have to suffer for his sexual perversion.

The door to the room opens up. He's here. I take a deep breath and prepare to meet my killer. As he turns the light on, I can see various instruments of torture hung on the wall. Drills, saws, knives, screws, hammers, scalpels, razor blades, needles, duct tape… I wonder what he'll use on me…

As he grabs a drill and inserts a long, pointed bit, I can only prepare for what will happen next. He starts it up and ploughs it right through my left thigh. The pain is immense. I try to scream but no sound escapes my mouth. I can feel it twisting my flesh up, churning my muscles and digging deep to my femur. As he reaches the bone, I can feel it all the way to my teeth. My head starts to pound heavily and I can feel the vomit rising from my stomach and out of my mouth.
He retracts the drill from my leg and places it back on the table. Just when I think he's done, he grabs one of the hammers. Coming back towards me, he sticks the end used to remove nails into my leg wound. I can feel him stripping the flesh of my thigh and now I know what a pig at a slaughterhouse feels like.

I wish I could see his face, but the mask he's wearing prevents me from doing so. It's a severed goat's head with holes in the eye sockets and the lower jaw missing. Though I can't see his full face, I can see the sadistic and crooked smile forming on it.

I call him Goat-face, just because that's all I know him as, I remember meeting him in the bar but to tell you the truth I was way out of it, so to actually remember what he looks like without the mask on is – well very vague. I do remember us having sex but after that nothing.

God my head hurts.

This bastard's been killing people for God knows how long and for what?

For pleasure?

I wish I could see this sicko's face. Just so I could get some closure as to who killed me. I wish I could gaze into the eyes of this goat fucker and then rip them out with my bare hands.

My thoughts distract me from the pain, but not for long. I can see that he's stripped the majority of the flesh off of my leg. All that's left is a bloody mass of twisted muscle and bone. He approaches the table again and grabs what appears to be a lemon. With one of the rusty kitchen knives, he cuts it in half and dips it in a bag of salt.

"Oh fuck you! Fuck you, you goddamn cunt! I'll fucking kill you!"

He laughs. He thinks this is funny. That all of this is for his amusement. That human lives are nothing but toys for him to play with until he gets tired of them.

He approaches me slowly, salted lemon in hand. He squeezes it and lets some of the juice fall into my wound. I let out a shriek of pain. This guy really knows how to add insult to injury. The lemon starts to approach my leg. Slowly, cautiously, precisely, he sticks the euthanized citrus fruit onto my exposed muscles. The pain is so intense. It feels like a thousand needles stinging my leg. And if that weren't enough, someone had passed a blowtorch over my leg.

As I scream out in pain, he pulls his pants down and starts masturbating. His moans mixed with mine are a variable orchestra of perversion and disgust. It makes me want to bleed from my ears. He twists in spasms of pleasure and ecstasy while I twist and squirm in pain. His tongue escapes his mouth and licks his lips, and as his sticky, white juices escape the shrinking limb in his hand, he collapses onto a chair.

He pulls his pants back up and approaches the table. He grabs a knife and comes towards me. He approaches his face to mine and whispers in my ear.

"I don't need you anymore."

He raises the knife and pulls his mask off. As he slits my throat, I gaze at his face. I'll never forget it. It was a face twisted in sadism and murder. A face filled with evil and contempt. It was the face of a mass murderer.

I carried out the work as I saw through her eyes, I woke her up and made her realise where she was and what was going to happen to her.
Then I did it, the drill, the lemon, the lot.
As she bled out, I removed the shackles and she slumped to the floor, time for stage three:

Dismember.

I got my cordless jigsaw (great value £29.99 out of B&Q) and set about removing her legs and arms.

I think her name was Evelyn, oh well who gives a flying fuck!

Not me that's for sure.

I cut through her neck and blood flowed like red wine, oh how it felt as though I was covered in blackcurrant Ribena juice!

I placed the head, arms and legs to one side and picked up the body of the girl, I held it tight and as the moonlight shone outside, I danced around the room with the carcass as her internal organs spilled to the floor. (It's amazing the length of the human intestines!)

After a few moments of my dance of death, I cleaned up and placed my newest trophy into various bags – it was time to take her to her new living area.

Room 4, as I opened the door and walked in with the body in black bags (or as I like to say the body-bag! Ha) I dumped her on the bed then walked back to door.

"Sleep tight my darling; you are going on a long trip to the bottom of the loch later."

I closed the door.

I walked along to room 3 and opened the door –

THE SCALPED BITCH WAS STILL ALIVE!

I raced over to her, "Why won't you die!" I screamed as I pulled out my Stanley blade from my back pocket and plunged it deep into her throat.

Now she's dead.

I left the room and went outside onto my front door step, I breathed in, taking in the fresh night air and then I felt the pain in my stomach, I looked down and a small circular patch of a red stain was forming.

Blood?

I looked around, dazed and confused then I saw standing to my right was someone in the shadows. I saw him cock his head to one side.

He stepped out of the shadows and smiled at me.

"There is only room for one modern day Jack the Ripper and you're not him!"

He raised his scalpel and ran it across my throat, blood poured out and down I went onto my knees, I saw him walk down the steps into the still of the night.

He turned around and smiled, "You'll know my name as Jacob Kane!"

I closed my eyes and fell into the abyss along with all my victims.

MY BEST FRIEND - DEAD

"Don't you die on me!" I screamed and screamed, "I need you, come back to me for fuck-sake!" He still didn't hear me.

I'll start at the beginning, my best friend or Daddy as I liked to call him was having chest pains. He was in with me myself. In the living room, he was resting, his wife had taking him to hospital the other day where as I came to know he was just told he had the flu and was just to relax for a few days and don't go to work just stay in the house. So he listened and stayed in. His wife went out to her mums for New Year's dinner leaving him alone. I said I would take care of him and that I did until he stood up clutched his chest and collapsed. I swear I could hear his heart beat fast and then stop. It was without a shadow of a doubt a heart attack. (I've watched enough ER programs to know what it looks like!)

He collapse in front of the coffee table, "Please come back to me," I screamed, "I need you, I'll die if you don't come back to me."

My stomach was rumbling, I was hungry, but I could leave my best friend. He took me in and I swore that I would lay by his side until the day I die or he dies (I just wasn't expecting it to be today!)

He took his last breath and that was him - dead.

My best friend was dead. My daddy dead.

Hours pasted and I lay next to him, cuddled him but my stomach still yelled for food.

Now you would say, 'Why didn't I phone the emergency services? Why didn't I call his wife? Why didn't I get food from kitchen?'

Answers soon, I assure you.

The hunger pains toppled me over, I needed to eat. So I did - I turned to my, 'Daddy,' and started eating at his face, the soft grizzled texture of his cheek tasted salt, a bit like chicken. I fed and fed on my best friend's body, it tasted so good, the blood dripping from my mouth as I flicked my tongue out to lap it up like milk.

"I'm sorry again Daddy," I said, "but I had to eat." I finished off his body exposing the bone beneath as I lay next to him; I heard the keys turning in the front door lock and in walked his wife right into the living room. She screamed as she saw the body of her husband, screamed as she saw my face covered in the blood of her man.

"You stupid, stupid bitch!" She shouted at me, "you stupid cat!"

Yes I'm a cat!

Now you know why I couldn't call someone or make my dinner.

I purred at her as she raised her hand and slapped me.

I fed on my daddy, my owner and it's my fault she screamed.

If only I could tell her he had a heart attack!

DON'T MESS WITH THIS STREET

"Have you ever danced with the devil in the pale moonlight?" that's a question that I always refer to when something happens.

Drumchapel is my playground, my home. I was born and bred in Drumchapel, Glasgow and it will always be in my heart. Now to move on to more pressing matters, there is a boy that terrorizes this one street in particular, a street called Kilcloy Avenue.

I found out his name was Brian Driver, you see he acts like a wee hard man, shouting abuse at young and old people. Boys and girls. Men and woman. Well I certainly wasn't going to let this little, 'boy,' get away with terrorizing my home town.

I got the call off of a concerned citizen with regards to this little prick. "Please can you help us? He gets away with it all the time. The police don't do anything. He's fifteen years old."

I sighed, "What does this guy look like?"

The concerned neighbour sighed back at me down the receiver, "You'll know him as soon as you see him, just be at Kilcloy Avenue, you know the lane that runs along the school to St Marks Church? Be there tonight and you'll see him. Around 7pm he walks along passed the houses shouting abuse at the neighbours in their houses. There is one neighbour who has a Labrador, this dog can sense people that are bad and barks at him all the time. You see he recently threatened a family with a knife and the police are not doing anything! So can you help?"

I cleared my throat, "Of course I can!" I hung up the phone and walked into my bedroom, it was time to, 'suit up,' so to speak.

I pulled on my black combat trousers, my red and green jumper (stripy – good for concealing) my black hooded top and my black baseball cap. I went into the kitchen and grabbed my, 'home-made,' weapon or weapons to be precise. It was 8 knives that I taped to my fingers. (Get the picture now!?!)

I left and made my way to the lane at the church. It was a dark and damp night, I hid in the bushes just across from Kilcloy Avenue and waited, I looked at my watch, 18:59pm and then as it hit 19:00pm along comes this boy all alone, all by himself. I waited until he passed by me and then I stepped out behind him.

"Brian, Brian Driver?" I spoke in my fake raspy voice.

He turned round, "Yeah who's asking?"

I smiled, "Have you ever danced with the devil in the pale moonlight?"

A confused look came over him, "What the fuck are you saying?"

I smiled, "Have you ever danced with the devil in the pale moonlight?" I asked him again.

He turned and began walking away from me, "Go to fuck you old bastard, or I'll stab you!" and there it was, the threat, the action of a knife.

I walked fast up to him and spun him round, "Do you know who I am?" I asked him.

He cocked his head to one side and spat on the pavement, "Yeah a fucking poofter!" he laughed.

I raised both my hands and revealed in the moonlight my weapons. My knives for fingers. His face was a picture only a mother would love!

"Whoa, whoa, whoa mate look I was only joking!" He backed away from me.   But I moved forward towards him. "Listen to me little boy, I am God and I tell you what to do, you don't threaten people, I threaten people. Now you go and play fetch with your doggy and if I see you in this neighbourhood again, I'll gut you like a fish – understand?"

He gulped and nodded and began backing away, I turned and that's when I felt the cold steal enter my back just next to my kidney, the pain was excruciating, I spun round and the pain in the ass stood in front of me with the knife dripping of my blood onto the damp pavement. I looked up and saw people, neighbours, looking out at the scene on their streets.

He smiled at me, "this is my town bitch and I am God!" he declared.

I smiled and pointed my knives for fingers to over his shoulder. He looked confused and then turned only to be confronted by a black Labrador, bearing his teeth at the little boy. I swear I'm sure he wet himself!

The dog (built like a tank) steadily walked towards Brian and Brian backed up towards..........me. He backed right into me and spun round to face me, this time he dropped the knife and I raised my weapons and drove them deep into his stomach. He screamed an almighty scream and tears streamed down his face. He backed off of my knives and fell to the ground, only to be confronted by the black Labrador staring down at him, the dog growled a deep hateful growl and bent its head down and tore the thugs throat out. Blood pooled around the dying boy, I went over to the dog and patted it on its side, and it jumped up on me, "Good boy, such a good boy."

"Well done," I heard from across the street, followed by a roar of cheers and whistles. I looked up and saw an old man walk over the road towards me, the dog and the dead thug.

"Well done son!" the old man said to me.

I nodded, "What's the dogs' name?"

The old man smiled, "We call him Tyson or Ty for short!"

I smiled and laughed, "No more pain here, listen if I'm not here then you have a good watcher of this street, I maybe the, 'fixer,' but he is the true GOD!" I walked away down the lane to a round of cheers and applause. Kilcloy Avenue was now a safe zone in Drumchapel.

Wherever there is trouble, just call me – the fixer.

TAKE A PICTURE IT LASTS LONGER

She stood there across the road from me, not known I was there.

She stood there across the road from me, while I watched her with that - that guy.

I always dreamed I would get my revenge, and I knew the day would come eventually, I just wasn't expecting it to be this soon.

I suppose I'll start from the beginning, I loved her with every ounce of life inside and she done this to me. It happened just 2 weeks ago, that I walked in on her with this guy, (and no she wasn't having sex - before you jump to conclusions!) I told her don't go and do this you will regret it, but 2 weeks later I'm witnessing it first-hand.

Rage more than anything came over me (did me a young 8 year old boy have that guts to go over there and tell her?)

Nope I instead followed them as they walked to the car park. Back to his car I presumed. I walked at a steady pace behind them both making sure not to be seen.

I saw them get in his car and just before she climbed in, I ran up and pulled out the black handled kitchen knife - I drove it deep into her neck and twisted it and then pulled it out (I must have hit the carotid artery because blood pumped out like a hose pumps out water!) He came running round the side of the car and tried to grab me but I was too fast for the idiot, I swung the blade round catching him across the throat (he was bent down anyway) blood poured down him and I smiled.

"Well mum I did say don't get back with dad didn't I?"

DON'T SCREW WITH ME

What happened to her? She died. I sent her to the grave myself. Stupid cunt, it didn't take long for me to know her double-sided nature. But I corrected her, and she died.

A whore doesn't deserve my sympathy, nor any love from me. Even after I did everything to make her happy, she went and dumped me like a used tissue.

Her screams were lilting harmonies to my ear, while I ripped into her skin like fresh construction paper. Frankly, killing can be quite artistic, you should try it sometime.

And there was that fuck-face of a man that was bedding her, a hatchet to the face made quick work out of him. It's also interesting to note how long a human being can live, all the while producing every shriek of agony that humanity could muster. Like I said before, it's all music to me.

You wouldn't believe a myriad of colours and shapes existed within the human body. My first glimpse was after she took her last breath, shards of a vase stuck deep within her throat. Oh, how she cried for help, how it made me giggle inside. While her heart still beat…I tore her belly open, and the magic of it all…!

Several handfuls of rose petals in her mouth soon took care of all distractions, and made lovely work embossed against the stench of her dying body. Entrails, viscera, whatever you would like to call it, strewn about all over the living room of her apartment in bloody streamers, like some perverse birthday party for the leader of a Satanic cult.

She deserved it; don't look at me like that. After all, she wasn't exactly going through any guilt trips while getting ploughed by that bastard in the bedroom, although…………his face wasn't quite recognizable anymore.

Her blood was still hot with the desperation and will to survive. How do you like it on the other side, bitch? The grass isn't green, but bloody here. Love, what a fucking joke. However, her intestines do make for a few hours of interest.

Her boyfriend……he was ugly on the outside, and my suspicions were correct. He's fucking ugly on the inside too. I crushed his heart first, the most despised organ of my eyes. No man would have the gall to ever do what he just did, and he didn't deserve this organ of dignity. It popped, like a squishy, red balloon. Blood coursed down my forearms, and the sheer delight of the moment ran through me again. Hell, you could say I was getting rocks off this stuff.

Disgusted? Maybe…that part of me died when I first learned about her affair. But in the end…all I felt was happiness while I threw around what little remained of my fiancée all over the apartment, chastising her only out of the sheer love I had for her.

I'm not crazy… I merely try too hard. They both got what was coming to them, and now they're dead. It's none of my fault…it was theirs.

But anyway…back to my magical fable.

Many hours were spent…and you could say I did make a couple love stains on their corpses, but hey, time flies when you're having fun, am I right?

In the end, the tissues of her face were nothing but bloated and beginning to reek with the slow encroachment of rot. I still loved her at that moment, even though she really let herself go. She should think about going on a diet.

As for the boyfriend, I just jammed all of his shit down the toilet, the sink, and dropped everything else in the bathtub. Fuck him, who does he think he is? He didn't even have the decency to die like a normal human being. He cried like an animal while I was carving his face like a Thanksgiving turkey. I distinctly remembered an eye popping out, and watched it roll along the bedroom floor. It looked much like a marble, although with a growth that resembled the root of a sapling. Even through my own bloodshot eyes, I could still see that the root was throbbing, beating away its last pulses of life.

I brought down the heel of my foot on the round thing, and felt it give way with a sickening plop, reddish-pink piles of flesh spewing out of the surprisingly hard object.

I thought of jawbreakers then, and giggled while wiggling the cleaver out of his face. I made short work of his genitals and squeezed his scrotum until it popped, like when you put something too long in a microwave. Warm jizz coated my arm, already leaving fashionable stains on my arms. His penis I burned on a skillet in the kitchen, and watched it curl up and die, just like my hopes and dreams.

I made sure he could find his old self if he ever looked from Hell. I'm sure that right now, he's down there and screaming in agony. That brings a smile to my face, it really does. As for my fiancée, I grew bored of her silence and unwillingness to repent. I did what any loving person would do. I smashed her skull in with a picture frame. Ironically enough, the picture was our trip to Switzerland three months ago. The smiling, upbeat woman I adored now had no face, the basic model for the human countenance now running and smeared all over the couch.

By then, the ferocious red-blue glare of police lights caught my eye, and I gladly waved them in, to show them my wonderful fiancée's home. Needless to say, they weren't ecstatic like I was, and now I find myself here.

The trial was a breeze. I only sat there and smiled while the judge condemned to life in prison (probably be out in 35 years. Europe, you got to love the Human Rights!) I even recall telling him that I fucked his mother. That really put a spring in his step. I also recall several guards pulling me back from him, the gavel whistling just inches from my face. They really ought to lock psychos like him up.

I hear the faint footsteps of a guard. They promised me a friend will be joining me soon, some other wank-stain that apparently killed his wife because she slept with someone else. Ooohhhh how we will have so much fun comparing notes – NOT!

There it is, my last present for this year. Out goes 2014, here comes 2015!

As I sit here in my small cell on my bunk watching SKY TV and drinking my freshly brewed cup of tea, I ponder the old subject –

Was it worth it?

Damn right it was worth it!

Three square meals a day, exercise and I get to study for qualifications. (Not bad for a killer.)

Don't get me wrong, I loved my fiancée, but she screwed the wrong guy (literally.)

So now I reside in this place I call home along with another fucker, watching Deal or no Deal.

Get in there!

THE VISION I SAW

It had all started pretty normal. Just got out of bed like any other day, quick wash, got ready, and set off out. It was both mine and my wife's day off. We were going into Glasgow City Centre, for a shop around (buying new stuff to do up our flat.) We waited on the number 204 to arrive to takes us into town and once it arrived, we jumped on. We sat down in the middle of the bus.

Then it started to go horribly wrong. I should have known something wasn't quite normal when I got on the bus, I got this feeling in the pit of my stomach and someone shouting in my head it's going to happen today. But I shook it all away and sat down in at the window with my wife sitting in at the aisle.

I should have listened to my gut. Anyway, I actually got to read the free newspaper which comes on the UK transport network called, 'the metro,' and while my wife played, 'Angry Birds,' on my phone we both minded our own business. I read the sports pages first, about my beloved Rangers football club and the sorry state it's in at the moment, when all of a sudden I hear an almighty horrendous scream come from the back of the bus.

He was about 19 years old, 6 feet tall or so, and holding a very large knife. He had what looked like some sort of bomb (I'd say) strapped to his chest and stomach. Blood dripped from the knife, and as the rest of the passengers began looking round they noticed at least four other passengers stabbed to death. Blood soaked the aisle, soaked the windows. This guy was going crazy, wielding this knife, swinging it back and forward as if it was a baseball bat.

He moved quickly down to the front of the bus slashing people as he went, I pulled my wife into me and tried to shield her as best as I could. There was no denying it I was scared!

This psychopath got to the front of the bus and (literally) pulled the drivers cabin door off of its hinges. He thrust the knife into the drivers face and all we heard was, "You stop – I kill all – tick, tick, tick, BOOM!"

People screamed louder and I swear, I watched out the corner of my eye as I saw the emergency door at the back of the bus swing open and people jumping from the moving bus. We were on the motorway now and the driver had to abide by the speed limit and not stop as instructed by this psycho brandishing the knife at him.   Kids screamed, adults cried, and blood poured. I was brave but wasn't that brave. Not brave enough to stand up to a maniac and be cut literally into tiny bits. So I sat cuddling my wife telling her I love her over and over again. She said the same back through teary eyes.

The emergency door was swinging open then close, bang, bang, BANG it went as more people threw themselves onto the road. Cars swerved trying to avoid the falling people, but unfortunately all I heard (and saw) was bodies being splattered left, right and centre on the road. Then I heard sirens, yes the police were in pursuit, they were swerving through the wreckage of bodies and cars across the motorway. I whispered to my wife to give me a pen, she searched her bag and pulled a pen out. I wrote on the newspaper in big writing, 'BOMB,' and stuck it up to the window as the police car pulled alongside. I watched as the shocked police officers went white as a sheet.
I knew they were thinking terrorist attack, but surely not.

This guy was just a nutcase, a few marbles short, insane maybe but couldn't be a terrorist.

Could he?

This guy wasn't though. He just stood there shouting tick, tick, BOOM! He told the driver to speed up and the driver did just that. That freaked me out the most. He looked up at the carnage he caused and smiled, then ran up to the centre of the bus, (just across from me and my wife) and began stabbing and old man in around the head.

Screams continued and he turned and smiled and then screamed the words, "For Christ our almighty, the end is not nigh, the end is now!" He flicked a switch and within seconds we heard a faint beep, beep, beep noise. Then he shouted, "Goodbye, may the Lord have mercy on your souls!" and with that came the BOOM he kept going on about.

The bus blew up from the inside to the outside, shards of metal and fabric flew through the air as did my wife, I couldn't hold onto her as she flew out of my arms, I watched as she disappeared into the blackness, people all around me started to burn up in flames, a kid in front of me screamed loud as a pole that held the seat to the roof came loose and impaled her through the left shoulder. Men, women and children, old, young and now dying alongside me on the bus from hell.

The maniac was gone in sixty seconds splattered across the windows along with the other passengers; I still remember his smile before he flicked the switch.

Then I felt the burning sensation, I looked at my hands and saw my skin and flesh begin to melt away. My bones exposed, my wedding ring fell to the ground of the exploded bus and rolled away into the blackness where now my wife resided. I reached my one good hand up to my head and when I brought it back down again a clump of my forehead came with it, my skin was peeling away exposing all my bones beneath as though the bomb that went off had some sort of acid in it.

I screamed but no words came out, then I lost my vision and I was now in the blackness.

HELL HAS A HOME

I am a security guard watching after an insurance building. One hot summer's night I was working nightshift when something happened to me.

This is my story.

It was May 29th 2015; I had just begun my nightshift at work after getting my hand-over from the day guard. He told me not to enter the roof gardens as an incident happened there at 10am this morning. I quizzed him on what had happened, but he refused to tell me. All he said was, "see the contractors that were in – well the scaffolding they were on collapsed!" I was gob-smacked; this scaffolding was on the 9th floor almost 500 feet up in the air, towering above Glasgow City Centre, overlooking Waterloo Street and Douglas Street.

The day guard left and yet again told me, "Remember the roof gardens are out of bounds!" I nodded and locked the door as soon as he had left. It was to be a long night as no staff were to come in due to the incident, the building was closed. So I was now alone.

Only one thing to do……investigate!

I called the lift and headed up to the 9th floor. Got out and turned to my left, I opened the double doors and stepped out into the hot fresh air of the summer night. All around me lay the twisted steel of the scaffolding. I was amazed. I walked around the gardens looking at all the mess, the cracked slabs, the ripped apart slates on the wall; it was as though I was in the middle of a disaster movie or the equivalent of Afghanistan.

I walked around peering at everything when something caught my eye just to the right of me. I walked over to the safety barrier (yeah that's what the call tube steel pipes cemented into the wall!) where it's so easy for you to climb over or under and stand on the ledge of the roof or indeed jump if you so wish.

Anyway I investigated the thing that caught my attention, there was in front of me a hard hat and underneath it a dark thick pool of blood.

"What the hell!" I mumbled out, "what the hell happened here?" obviously talking to myself, (had a strange way of doing that lately!) I decided to investigate further and climbed under the safety barrier because the blood below the hard hat was trailing out to the ledge. (Don't worry I love heights so not scared at all.)

I followed the trail out and peered over the ledge, there hanging from a loose slate was what appeared to be a body of a man (well what was left of him anyway!)

"What the hell happened here?" I quizzed to thin air, "why wasn't this body moved by emergency services?" still as always no-one talked to me.

I backed away from the body and clambered back over the barrier into, 'safety ground,' I decided it was best to call the building manager first, so out came my mobile phone and then I dialed and it rang and rang and rang, then I felt it, the warm sensation of a liquid pour down the back of my neck soaking my blue shirt, I looked down and noticed it wasn't just any liquid it was blood…………my blood!

I spun around quickly and felt another stabbing pain as this time my arm was cut badly by a knife which seemed to pierce my skin and stick right into my bone. Blood now gushed from my head and my arm and standing in front of me was……………The dayshift guard!

He cocked his head to one side, "I told you this place was out of bounds, but did you listen? No you didn't! You decided to investigate. Well this is what happens to people who investigate." He raised a metal pole (probably from the scaffolding) and brought it down on my head, I felt my skull and head meat crush together and felt the blood pour out of my ears, nose and eyes. This guy was killing me!

I stumbled back and fell to the ground as another blow came from the steel pipe. This time to my ribcage, bones cracked, blood poured and skin ripped like cellotape.

I watched as he smiled then it all came back to me as I slowly faded away to my death.

I saw the collapse of the scaffolding, the dayshift guard showed me what happened, he walked out onto the roof gardens and actually loosened a few bolts while a worker was on top. The scaffolding fell collapsing in a heap on the roof causing the worker to fall to his death, the dayshift guard smiled an evil smile and then walked away.

And now I lay here dead, his second victim (I think!) God only hopes I'm his last.

MY GARDEN, MY BEAUTIFUL GARDEN

My garden, my beautiful garden, I landscaped it myself. The lawn nice deep green colour; surrounded by white pebbles and set off with different flowers and plants.

My garden, my beautiful garden, no one and I mean no one messes with my garden.

Just ask Jim the local police officer, he messed with my garden. He stepped onto my grass and I – well I cut his ass up into little tiny chunks. He's now residing underneath my rose bush (wish my dear old mother-in-law gave me as a gift.)

Did you know the human bodies skin, meat and bodily fluids is actually really good fertiliser?
Seriously, obviously don't ask another gardener or your neighbour – just take my word for it. I've been using human bodies (well sometimes just pieces of them) for years now. I kill people just so I've got enough fertiliser to last for a while.

This one time my next door neighbour poked his bloody head over our dividing fence and cackled, "Hey Tommy where did you get that fertiliser? It seems to be working a treat!" I called him over, but the stupid idiot jumped over the fence instead of walking round to my garden gate! He jumped over my fence and landed right on my rose bush! I cursed him under my breath, how dare he ruin my garden, my beautiful garden.
Well after I saw what he did, a pair of garden shears came into my hands, and while he began to stand up and turn to me, the garden shears went around his fat neck and with one quick cut; dear old Peter had his head chopped off!

More fertiliser for my beautiful garden.

The local Council garden contest is coming up and I know I will win. My garden is the most beautiful garden out of the whole neighbour.   Yeah so there are a few skeletons underneath my soil – but everyone has skeletons in their closet, I just so happen to bury mine!

This one time my wife (God rest her) was helping me lay red bark below the window of the living room. I planned on a colour scheme one year, you see the house is red bricks with a hint of white so what I was planning was red bark with white pebbles followed by more red bark then it was the green grass. But you know what she did, my idiotic wife, well she put white pebbles then red bark then white pebbles again.

I screamed and screamed and screamed, "No, no, NO!" at her, but would she listen eh well, NO!!! She wouldn't stupid bitch. So late one night, I grabbed hold of my garden spade and while she sat drinking her tea at the kitchen table, I raised the spade and whacked her over the head with it. Dazed and confused she dropped her tea and it spilled everywhere around her and then she fell to the ground, shaking uncontrollable, then the blood pooled underneath her mixing in with the warm tea.

I disposed of her by digging a hole in the middle of the garden and planting a lovely green fern tree on top of her.

Don't get me wrong police questioned me intensely about her disappearance but I got cleared, (maybe it was due to me copying her handwriting and sending a letter to her mother in Ireland, saying I left Tommy due to his obsessive disorder with his bloody garden!) Police didn't question me any longer. They put it down to marriage break-up and the fact she didn't want to be found. Easy killing there if I do say so myself!

Oh here come the judges now, I'm so excited, that I nearly peed myself with such happiness. The judges are next door, looking at my dearly departed neighbours' garden. Eh hello I'm the only one that takes care of my garden, my beautiful garden.

Ah finally, here they come now, entering my garden and looking about. I'm standing on my front step with a big smile and my hands clasped firmly behind my back, I'm so proud of what I have done to my garden, that I know I have one first prize.

They are walking around admiring my plants and my green fern tree. Wait why are looking so disgusted?

Then I hear them whispering to each other, "Is that a tooth?" I hear one say then, "Oh my God that's a foot!"

They look at me in horror, why I don't know maybe it's something to do with the intestines decorating my green fern tree in the middle of my garden?

Maybe it's the skull lanterns that hang from my houses walls?

Or maybe it's the fact I am standing there covered in blood eating the heart of my wife?

I can hear the police coming now, the sirens in the distance. It won't be long until I'm finally locked up for good.

But that can't happen to me, what about my garden, my beautiful garden?

"No, no, NO!" I scream as the police drag me across my green grass, trailing me through my plants as they squash below me.

I shed a few tears in front of the jury a few weeks later, as the judge announces I'm a wee bit cuckoo in the head. Cries of, "kill the bastard," come from the viewing gallery.

But now I reside in Carstairs, (it's not home but they do let me landscape the gardens.)

My gardens, my beautiful gardens.

GARTNAVEL

I ran through the empty wards of the hospital, ran for my life, ran from the man behind me, I came to call him the man but to tell you the truth - I never saw, 'the man,' I never knew, 'the man,' and I sure of hell didn't want to ever meet the man!

I passed by empty cells, yes cells, padded cells; I was running through the, 'mental,' bit of the hospital. Home of just the crazy people. We always joked, (me and the rest of the patients) you can sign in but never sign back out.

I was in and certainly wasn't getting back out. Room after room I passed until I came to one room, the door was locked and the room was in total darkness. I stopped and took a step towards the small window. I peered in and then jumped back as.......Inmate 21456 or Emma as we got to know her came screaming, yelling towards the door.

"Let me out, let me out," she screamed and screamed. Banging on the steel door, "please let me out, he's coming - the man is coming!"

I backed away, looked down the corridor - he was nearing us, nearing me. Hell Emma was safe stuck in the padded cell (crazy that she was!) Me I'm stuck out here with the man, he was coming.
I muttered, "Sorry," and turned and hot footed it away from Emma and the man. I ran and ran and then I heard the scream. I turned around and Emma's cell door flew off its hinges, then the blood flew out, followed by limbs, Emma was being slaughtered and I didn't help her.

I muttered again, "I'm sorry." But hot-tailed it again followed by the man again.

He screeched along the corridor towards me and then out of nowhere, I was pulled into another cell.

"Sshh," came the voice out of the darkness and from behind me. I turned and stared into the darkness.

"Who are you?" I whispered.

"Who are we, you mean?" the voice told me.

"Then who are you both?" I asked.

"My name is Leah and this is Katie, we are here to help battle the man!" One voice said (apparently Leah)

"Yes here to help you Daniel" the other voice stated (Katie I guessed)

"How?" I asked. But all I was met with was laughing then grunting and followed by screaming then I was overcome with blood.

Blood covered me from head to toe - the man was in the dark cell with us!

The man had butchered the two people who were going to help me and I stood there and done nothing again!

"Arghhh," I screamed as this time I wasn't going to run. I ran at the man and quickly ran into the wall. The man had bloody disappeared!

Emma - dead, Leah - dead and Katie - dead. I was simply all alone, then I saw him - I saw the man, he stood basking in light at the end of the corridor. He didn't seem evil or a monster anymore; he seemed peaceful almost like an angel. He gestured for me to go to him. I began walking slowly towards the man, as I neared him I put my hands out to hug my saviour and the man done the same, his hands came up in sync with mine.

I got closer and closer, I was about to see the man for the very first time.

Five, four - closer I got.

Three, two - closer.

And one, here I was in front of the man........in front of me.

I stared at the mirror in my cell, my room and knew the doctors were watching through the glass. I couldn't see them but they watched me.

"Here is a patient who plays out the murder of his sisters' day in and day out. Daniel claimed that the man killed them but the man was in fact his other persona, the man was David." The doctor said, I could hear them but never saw them, "too dangerous," they said, "nut job," they said, "mind of a madman," I heard them call me.

    My name was Daniel, and I was a writer……once.

HAPPY KILL

"When I first saw you, I saw love. And the first time you touched me, I felt love. And after all this time, you're still the one I love."

We drove along the road, she didn't speak to me once, just gave me the silent treatment. I thought I would take her to the most romantic place, a place where we first met.

"Looks like we made it. Look how far we've come my baby. We might have taken the long way, but we knew we'd get there someday!"

Still silence from her, what did I do wrong? Maybe I would never find out.

"They said I bet they'll never make it. But just look at us holding on, we're still together still going strong."

I put my foot down and sped up but began to cry, "You're still the one. You're still the one I run to, the one that I belong to. You're still the one I want for life. You're still the one that I love. The only one I dream of. You're still the one I kiss good night!"

We got closer to our romantic place, the old pier at Loch Lomond. The darkness and cold was setting in as we pulled up. She still didn't speak to me. "Look," I began, "Ain't nothing better, we beat the odds together. I'm glad we didn't listen, look at what we would be missing"

I got out the car and went round the side of it. I opened up the boot and pulled my wife out of it, dragging her body along to the pier. It was dark and no one was insight. I sat down curling my feet underneath me and placed my wife's head on my lap. I stroked her blood matted hair, tears formed in my eyes but I remained strong, known this was the end of us.

"You're still the one; you're still the one I run to. The one that I belong to. You're still the one I want for life. You're still the one that I love, the only one I dream of. You're still the one I kiss good night."

With that said I pushed her body into the Loch and watched for a few minutes before the body sank to the bottom of the Loch, down to the lost city beneath the water. I didn't want to kill her, but after discovering her in bed with my brother, I had no choice. I knew still that I couldn't live without her, so as I watched her sink, I stood up, produced the knife that I had in my jacket pocket – the one I used to slit both her throat and my brothers throat (he lay in my house bleeding out all over my freshly laid plush beige living room carpet.) I held the knife up and pulled it across my throat as well, blood oozed out down my white Armani shirt, dripping onto my Prada shoes, I fell to my knees before finally falling into the Loch myself, my life passed by my eyes fast as I fell into the abyss.

To me, she would always be the one.

BLOOD LADY IN RED

"You know I've never seen you looking as lovely as you did tonight Julie. I've never seen you shine so bright, I've never seen so many men ask you if you wanted to dance, they're looking for a little romance, given half a chance, and I have never seen that dress you're wearing, or the highlights in your hair that catch your eyes, I have been blind all this time, but now, now you are mine. For months I've wanted you and tonight, tonight I have you!"

She squirmed in the chair I had her tied on to. I didn't have her in a dungeon or in my attic or even in my basement; she was simply tied to my black leather recliner chair in the middle of my living room. Obviously I had my curtains and blinds shut, (I have a very nosey neighbour - old Mrs. Jefferies. Old bat needs put out her misery but first my Julie goes to the other side before her.

"Don't cry babe you'll get tear stains down your lovely dress. I always pictured you lady dancing with me, cheek to cheek, I pictured that nobody was there, it was just you and me, that's where I wanted to be. But now I hardly know this beauty in front of me. Now I'll never forget the way you look tonight."

More squirming, more tears falling, snot dripping out of her nose, make-up all smeared.

"Julie, I've never seen you looking so gorgeous as you are tonight; I've never seen you shine so bright, you are amazing, I've never seen so many people want to be there by your side, and when you turned to me and smiled, it took my breath away, and I have never had such a feeling, such a feeling of complete and utter love, as I do tonight. You are mine now Julie no one and I mean no one is going to come between us."

"Please Christian, let me go. I won't tell anyone, I promise," she mumbled.

I knelt down in front of her and shook my head, "One

word Julie - no. I'm not going to let you go, you are mine. I own you now."

I twirled the blade in my hand before slicing her throat open, blood poured down her, onto her white clinging dress. I stood back and watched the very essence of her life die out in her hazel brown eyes.

"I'll never forget the way you looked tonight.....my love, my lady, my lady in red."

I love you……maybe one day someone will write a song about you!

WHAT IS BLOOD IF NOT TO SHED?

    I moved back a few steps and pulled another chair from out of the corner of the room. I sat down.
    "I have nothing to hide, I've suffered and cried. But it's just made me tougher." I smirked as he squirmed in front of me.   "I've never mumbled and all the trouble I've been through has made me rise above it all, I've always had expectations that this day would come – in fact I've dreamed about this day, begged for it. Hell I got it inked on my body today's date. Look see!" I pulled down my polo shirt collar and showed him my neck:

                                        30-05-2015

    That was what was tattooed on my neck, the veins below it standing up and pulsing with anger.
    "You know when I was in prison, and you cut all ties with me, I wanted to vent the anger out in there but instead I said nothing at all. After all if I did anything in there, my sentence would have been extended and we didn't want that now did we?"
    He tried to get out of the make-shift shackles I had him in.
    "Family is something that you've never been to me, once you were but not in the past five years. So now, as you can see what with the camera set up and you in restraints, I am going to kill you. The camera footage is for people to discover, because let's face it in this day and age, everybody likes a little, 'found footage,' don't they?"
    I stood up and walked around the back of him, pulling his hair or what was left of it back so he was staring up at me.
    I pulled out a piece of paper. Unfolded it and read it out:

"Dear dad,
as a kid I looked up to you,
only thing was I never saw enough of you.
The last thing you said to me was you hated me.
To think, I used to blame me;
I wondered what I did to you to make you hate me.
I just wished you would have reached out.
I wish you would've been round when I'd been down.
But know that if I ever have kids;
unlike you I'll never let them be without me."

    I folded the piece of paper back up and then opened his mouth and forced the letter into his gapping mouth. I then grabbed duct tape and wrapped it round and over his mouth so he wouldn't spit it out.

    "Now dad, you're looking up at me!" I laughed as I took my knife and obliterated his throat by stabbing and slashing at it. Blood squirted out of him as though he was a fountain.

    As his life inched ever so closer to the darkness, I cocked my head to one side then I raised the knife and plunged it deep into his forehead right to the handle. I looked up and into the lens of the camera.

    "I'm not censoring myself for nobody. I'm the only thing I can be, all that is good, all that is bad, all that is me. Enjoy the movie!"

    I reached forward and stopped the tape.

DOOR 24

There is a door, a door that no one will go through, a door locked and padlocked so no one can get in. You'll find this door at the lower platforms of Glasgow Central Train Station. It has a plate on the door saying, 'Door 24,' no Network/Scot Rail staff member know what is behind that door.

Was it a doorway to the hidden street – Grahamston?

Or a doorway that was used for postal workers delivering mail to the boats on the Clydeside? One thing is for sure; whatever is behind door 24, it wants out……..soon.

JUNE 6TH 2015 – EARLY MORNING

Like any other commuter, Jim Shanks stood on the platform waiting on the train home. He got that bored as yet again three days in a row the great service from ScotRail was again running late. Probably a leaf on the track he thought laughing to himself. He sighed loud before turning and pacing back and forward along the platform. As he continued his legs exercise, he bypassed a door which was padlocked. Nothing strange there he thought but the way the number plate that was screwed into the door made him stop and look twice at it. The number plate was a bronze plate with silver engraved numbers on it, the number 2 and 4 – 24.

Jim looked about to see if anyone was watching him before he moved closer to the door and pushed it, soft at first then hard. Although it was padlocked, the door moved slightly, he could see a white light beyond the door through the crack. He looked about again and then pushed hard against the door again. This time the door gave way from underneath him and he fell through the door landing hard on the floor beyond the platform. As he got back up, he turned and stared out at the platform. The scene in front of him changed. It was surreal to him almost as though he was watching a silent black and white movie. The colour was drained from the platform, people walked about or sat about the platform but all were encased in black and white – then door 24 slammed shut in front of him.

He jumped as it banged. Surely someone heard it bang? He reached forward and grabbed the door handle and pulled at it trying to open the door up but it didn't budge. He knocked on the door but no one came towards the other side of the door. He couldn't hear anything at all from the platform side. He stepped back and then turned in the bright white light, he thought that the only way out must be through the white light. So he breathed in and out and began walking through the corridor that stood behind door 24. As he neared the middle of the white tunnel, he heard a noise. He looked behind, then to his left, then to his right and saw nothing but white light. He looked directly in front of him and then above him but still saw nothing. Then out of nowhere the whiteness of the corridor faded away and was replaced by blackness for a matter of a second before turning blood red in colour. Jim puzzled, continued to walk along the corridor which felt like it was never ending.

Where was he?

He heard stories of an old street-come-village called, 'Grahamston,' a place rich in history, part of the way Glasgow city centre use to be like until the expansion of the Caledonian Railway station later renamed Glasgow Central railway station which saw the demolishing of the street. Only two Grahamston buildings survived to this day that he recalls which are the Rennie Mackintosh Hotel in Union Street and the Grant Arms in Argyle Street.

He walked and walked then he heard it again the noise. From above, from the sides, from back of him, from in front of him. The noise was a screeching noise all around him, screeching, and scraping noise. All around him – on top of him. Puzzled, Jim ran along the corridor then the colour changed once again – from red to a deep amber colour. Jim shook his head in disbelief.

Why has no one came to door 24 yet?

Surely CCTV picked him up entering the corridor?

Questions ran through his mind and then -- THUMP!

He ran right into another door. No markings or numbers on this one though. He stepped back and then looked back behind him towards where the screeching scraping noise was. He decided he wasn't going to go back that way, so he turned to the new door and tried the handle. The handle stuck but after a few tries the door opened and in front of him, through the new door lay something completely different, something far from what he had just came from. The colours were dreary, dark, And Victorian almost.

He stepped through the door and out into – a street.

A street not familiar with him at all, a street rich in history. He knew he wasn't in Glasgow Central low level train station. Hell he knew he wasn't in Glasgow City Centre anymore. Well the Glasgow City Centre that he knew that was. He saw the street sign, it said, 'Alston Street,' and facing across from him was a theatre.

Alston Street?

Where the hell was he?

He turned around and looked at the door he came through.

It was a pub.

A pub called, 'Grant Arms,'

A person walked passed him wearing weird clothes – well weird to him as he was wearing jeans and a t-shirt!

However they were the ones that looked at him as though he was the weird one. He began walking along the street and passed by various thatched cottages. He felt amazed.

Did he travel back in time?

He passed a young boy; to Jim he looked homeless,

covered in dirt and grime. He stopped the young boy, "Hey kid where are we? What year is this?"

The young boy smiled and laugh, "Why sir this is Alston Street also known as Grahamston. The year is 1679. Where did you get your clothes sir?"

Jim laughed, "1679!?!"

"Well yes sir June 6th 1679," the young boy smiled.

"Thanks kid," Jim said putting his hand in his pocket and pulling out a crisp £10 note which he handed to the young boy. The kid looked at the, 'funny,' money and held it up to the light. "What is this sir?" the boy quizzed.

"It's gold dust son. Believe me hold on to it, put it somewhere safe and pass it down to each and every member of your family throughout the next few hundred of years." Jim told him. Then as the boy smiled a high screeching noise came from the direction that Jim came walking along from. Both him and the boy turned and looked and saw people running as though for their lives. The boy looked up at Jim, "Sir I suggest you run, and run now!"

"Why what's coming?" Jim asked but got no response as the boy ran away from him fast. People ran by him terrified, tears streaming down their faces. Jim just stood there watching the street become panic ridden.

What was going on?

The screeching noise continued and then Jim saw the shadow high above the street. The wingspan alone was really wide by his eyes he estimated something in the region of fifty feet of a wingspan.

"Run, run!!!!!" People shouted in unison as they bypassed him.

Jim grabbed hold of a middle aged well-dressed man as he ran by him screaming. "Hey, hey HEY!!!!! Who or even what the hell is that?" he looked and pointed up to the winged beast that towered above the street flapping its wings. "That young man is Abaddon the angel of destruction," the man told him, "Now run son run now and don't ever look back!"

"What does this……this Abaddon want?" Jim asked holding onto the man.   "Someone's soul," the man began, "Abaddon is from hell and if she doesn't get her soul, she will tear this street down and all that stands in her way!"

"Hell?" Jim began, "You don't believe in that crap do you? Demons? Supernatural? God? Heaven? Hell?"

"If we only believed in ourselves and that there wasn't something else lurking in the darkness then – well WHAT DO YOU CALL THAT? SCOTCH MIST?" the man yelled as he pointed to the winged demon that was poised to swoop down. The man wriggled free from Jim's grasp and began pounding the pavement as he ran away.

"Hey wait!" Jim yelled after him but he was gone leaving only Jim standing on the old street of Grahamston. Jim decided it was either fight or flight – he chose flight but instead of heading in the same direction of the public members, he decided to run back the way he came. Maybe it was stupid on his part but he knew he didn't belong in this place, this time, this era. He belonged in Glasgow, he belonged in the 21st century, he belonged in 2015 and he was going back there come hell or high water.

Hell – such an appropriate word for what was happening. Jim ran and ran back along Alston Street towards the pub known as, 'Grant Arms,' there he stood outside the door he came out of, listening to the flapping of the huge wings and the screeching, cawing of the demon called Abaddon. Jim tried the door handle but the door wouldn't budge, he then looked up at the winged monster as it starred down at him with its stone cold black beady eyes and with that stare came an almighty scream, "YOOOUUUUUU!"

Jim turned to the door and without hesitation, charged at the door with his shoulder – once, twice, three times before the door opened in front of him and he fell in and onto the floor of not the pub but the corridor of which he came from, he turned onto his back and watched as the winged demon swooped down and destroyed the street that he just stood in.

Abaddon couldn't get to him, couldn't fit her enormous wings through the tiny door, so he watched as the street came tearing down in front of him. Screeching noises, scrapping noises, loud bangs as timber and various other parts of the street came tumbling down. Jim stood up and reached forward to close the door, closing out the noise and the terror he had just witnessed. He then turned and began walking then running back along the corridor, back along the tunnel and out through the door marked, 'Door 24,' as he came to a stop out on the platform of Glasgow Central station. He rested his hands on his knees taking deep, deep breaths and then sat down on the floor. Commuters passed him and stopped to see if he was okay. A ScotRail staff member came rushing over to him, "Are you alright mate? Can I get you anything? Phone you someone?"

Jim stared up at him, breathed in and out and then spoke, "Do you know what happened to the old street that use to be here some four hundred years ago?" "Yeah Grahamston? Yeah it was demolished for the expansion of this train station." The young man told him.

"Wrong, the history books, the novels they are all wrong!" Jim told him, "And I know the truth!"

I WOULD DO ANYTHING FOR HER

She hung by her wrists, fully naked, her wrists tied up by cable ties which were then attached to a thick chain which was on a pulley system. Below her naked body lay a bucket.

I stood admiring her beautiful trimmed and toned body. She was a teenager, an eighteen year old brunette who knocked on the wrong door. I ushered her in, willing her to take a seat. She was selling some sort of household product (not that I was paying attention especially because she was wearing a short black skirt and a tight white blouse. To me it was the worst thing to wear especially if she knew who I was.

"Please......what are you doing? Please don't hurt me!" the young teenager pleaded while she hung by her wrists, thrashing about, trying to get down.

I admired her, I liked her and I needed her.

"Please let me go," she cried, "I won't tell. I promise I won't tell." Snot dripped from her nose, tears from her eyes and urine flowed from between her legs.

I smiled, "If only you knew." I turned and walked over to a cabinet that hung above a stainless steel sink; I opened it up and retrieved what was inside. I then returned to the girl, showing her what I had in my hands. She looked at it, although looked shocked more than anything.

"This is a photo of my daughter, she's beautiful isn't she?" I asked her. The girl gasped almost in horror, "She's......she's......" "She's beautiful isn't she?" I repeated, "Say it! Say that she's beautiful!" The girl cried, "But she's......she's......" "BEAUTIFUL!!!!!" I screamed. I raised my left hand and slapped her across the face, not once, not twice but three times. Blood trickled down her left cheek just below her eye the cut appeared. "My daughter is beautiful from the moment she was born, if you can't say anything nice, don't say anything at all!" I slapped her again.

"What do you want with me?" the girl cried again.

"My daughter has a skin disorder called, 'necrotising fasciitis,' it's a flesh eaten virus and well the doctors are done with skin grafts especially the doctors on the NHS and I simply can't afford to get her seen to privately……..soooooooo the next option is……well I take your skin for her!"   "No, no, NO!!!!" she screamed.

"Sorry the word is yes, yes, yes and you my beautiful young stranger, your soft beautiful tanned skin is just right for my daughter," I told her. I placed the photo of my daughter in my pocket and proceeded in picking up a scalpel from the metal tray that lay on the table next to the hanging naked girl. Then with precise surgical manoeuvres I began cutting the skin off the girl, layer after layer I peeled off of her, blood flowed and the girl went into shock. I lay the layers of skin on the table in a solution so it wouldn't dry out. I then began removing her face; I cut round the eye sockets and cut round the ears and the top of her forehead. I then peeled the skin down over her nose and placed it also in the solution.

I stood back and admired the hot naked girl in all her bloody glory. The muscles and veins that hid underneath the skin, the blood that pumped around the body, still flowed and now dripped from the body. A few minutes later whether it be shock or that she just woke up, she let out a mighty scream, I knew then and there I had to end her life, she was what? Seventeen years old maybe. It was time; I took the scalpel and slit her throat within minutes she bled dry.

Then came a knock at the door to my, 'Man's Cave,' I replaced the scalpel and walked over to the door. I opened it a bit and stared at my daughter – a young sixteen year old, the most beautiful girl that ever came into my life, I still don't understand why my wife, her mother walked out on this little cutie pie. "What is it sweetheart?"

"Just letting you know dad that the dogs are hunger and we haven't got any food in for them."

"Don't worry sweetheart," I told her. I opened the

door wide for her to see, "Got plenty now and got new skin for you!" I smiled.

She smiled back at me and it gave me a warm feeling inside, it made me happy to see her happy and I vowed till the day I die I would help her and always make her beautiful.

"Dad I love you!" she reached forward and kissed me.

"Love you too baby. Love you too."

TWISTED

I've been dreaming about her for a while now, in fact all my life. Ever since that day I met her on holiday in Corfu in 1996. When she got out of the pool in her black bikini, the water dripping from her long brown hair, dripping down and over her ample cleavage, oh her body, oh how I wanted her. I needed her and I was going to get her. I watched as she climbed out, stood next to her lounger and towel dried herself off, she made sure she got every bit of the water off of her. I watched intrigued, watched wondering how I was going to have her. It was though she was a pain in my neck, a thorn in my side; I just couldn't get her out my head......that was until I finally met up with her in Glasgow city centre. Can I just state for the record she contacted me through Facebook:

'Hey long time no see babe! Wanna meet up?'

Of course I wanted to meet up – I WANTED HER! So I agreed to meet her in Café Nero, it was a lovely Tuesday night, the first Tuesday in August and I sat there drink my large caramel latte when she entered and what an entrance she made. She wore tight white jeans and a low cut blue vest top – absolutely stunning. She ordered a coffee and we sat and chatted before we left together. We headed back to mine – oh how I've been dreaming of her, of this moment all my life, I always thought this wouldn't come true, she wouldn't come true – but she did.

Now when we got back to mine, before we even got through the front door she grabbed and pulled at me, pulled off my clothes and then we were on the floor of the living room making sweet love, the way I dreamed of it, then after twenty minutes it was over. The fire was over, the sweat was pouring from us, I wanted her and now I had her. She lay next to me, sleeping, naked. I closed my eyes......I must have been sleeping for what maybe twenty minutes when I heard this cracking noise.

Crack! Crack! Crack!

I fluttered my eyelids open trying to waken up from my lovely sleep.

Crack! Crack! Crack!

There it was again. I tried to sit up but for some reason I couldn't. I......I couldn't move.

What the hell?

Then I felt the pain, the pain on my body, I couldn't place where it was that was hurting until I looked down and saw where the pain was coming from. Pain in my neck – no. It was a thorn in my side, yes a thorn but not a thorn from a bush or a rose it was attached to a hand! My girls hand, the hand that attached to a beautiful body (not anymore!) the thorny hand attached to leather like skinned arm, I turned my eyes and stared at the girl beside me, her face had changed, she wasn't beautiful anymore, below her once beautiful brown eyes were thorn like things sticking out of her cheeks. Then her nose had stretched out to like a beak formation, her mouth and God her teeth had changed causing her beautiful teeth to change to razor sharp fangs. Then she arched her back while digging her thorn talon like fingers into my side, her back cracked and from her leather like skin came two wings.

I screamed and screamed and that's when she leaned in and with her razor sharp teeth she bit my tongue clean out of my mouth. I tried to scream but the blood filled my mouth and I reached up to the gaping hole that once held my tongue, blood poured down me and I fell back onto the floor. I was coming in and out of consciousness when she spoke.

"I'm sorry, but I need to feed every twenty years when we met on holiday in Corfu, in order for me to have that perfect body I......needed to eat a man, remember that barman Paul? How he went missing, that was me. I ate him, now twenty years later I have to do it again and you looked to good not to eat."

With that said I fell into the deep abyss that was darkness as I became the thing I once loved and wanted, the thing that I just had sex with, I call her the black widow.

Now total darkness engulfs me and I am no longer on planet earth.

A nightmare I will never waken up from.

Ever.

THE TRIPLE 6 KILLER

Have you ever taken a knife and pierced skin? Ripping deep down until you scrap the bone beneath?

He stood above his victim, a homemade mask concealing his identity. The papers and media called him, 'The Blender,' as he blended in with the public, no one knew him not until he was on them with his trusted knife, sticking and slicing them. He always made sure he stabbed them 66 times and then he carved a number 6 in the stomach of his victims. He hated being called, 'the blender,' he preferred, 'Triple 6 killer.' His victim shuddered underneath him as he knelt on top of her, he didn't mutter a word. He just stared through the emotionless red painted mask. He held the knife above her chest area. She cried as she knew it was the end of her life. She was simply another number to add to the list of murders that had taking place in Dalmuir Park. She tried to raise her arms to shield herself from more stab wounds but she was weak. The blood loss was bad, the cut on her stomach was so deep her intestines where trying to push out into the night air.

He raised the knife and with such force brought the knife down hard between the girls beautiful pert breasts forcing through her chest bone and piercing the heart below. Within minutes the girl was dead. His total victims to date were 65. He smiled underneath the mask before carving a number 6 in her body. He then arranged her body in such a way that it resembled Christ on the cross.

He stood up wiped his knife on his cloth he carried in his pocket. Before casually walking home for dinner with his loving wife and children.

MY HOUSE

"Welcome to my house, a house where no one comes back out. You won't find comfort in here, not now. Not ever."
I always wanted to be the best whoever did it. Live on forever telling people I made it. Like writing (I did it.) Like family (I made it.) Like killing people (I do it.) I want to be infamous beyond anything out there, I just don't know if that goal is feasible. But if it is well thank God for the gift he gave me.   I wrote for a newspaper, reporting on various stabbings, rapes and the occasionally murder now and again. Reporting just wasn't cutting it anymore, I wanted more.
I had a family, wife, two kids (Michael and Pamela) a dog (Freddy) and a cat (Jason) as you can probably guess I was also a horror nut. But I still wanted more.
I wanted to be the best out there. I studied various reports, studied various stories and came to the idea on what to do.
I just wanted to be the sickest guy stalking the streets and being as real as can be. Mayhem, sickness, murder and horror. These are the kind of words that describe my aura.
When I was a little boy I wanted to be a killer. Yeah I know – kids my age back then wanted to be police officers, astronauts, vets but look at them now, working for the council, on benefits or just junkies. But me I knew what I wanted to be. Yes so I became a reporter first and foremost, got a girl pregnant, got married, had a great wee house in a nice wee town. Well it was a nice wee town until murder and horror came crashing down on it. A killer stalked the streets (no not me) but I wished it was me. He descended on the town killing anyone and everyone, apparently he was out for revenge – his name was Zach Light.
I wanted to be him, this was my town, this was Drumchapel, I was born and bred in this town so I should have the infamy, not some low life that killed his brother and wanted revenge on his father for leaving him (oh boo fucking

hoo) Well at least I can kill in my house and no one bats an eyelid. My family don't know I do it and my neighbours don't know I do it.

See it's all about being stealthy, watch a few movies, and take a few notes (thank you Billy Loomis for your excellent one liner from Scream!) My basement was my own private place, the kids knew never to go down there and my wife knew as well. I had my projection screen and projector on one side where I had a three seater recliner and was able to watch my horrific horror movies by myself. On the near wall next to the screen stood a fridge and freezer, the fridge contained beer by the dozen and my beloved Irn Bru (oh how I loved my Irn Bru!) In the freezer well you would think it would contain ice cream and frozen ice lollies but sadly no, it contained body parts, girls' body parts mostly. You see while my wife was at work and my kids were at school, I roamed the streets, the alleyways and behind the shopping centre for girls. I then offered them a ride home. They all knew me as I was a reporter and accomplished writer. So they felt secure in my company.

I brought them here to my basement, locking the door they thought I liked them and wanted to have sex with them and believe me I am an actually nice catch if I do say so myself! However once they sat on my recliner and I started up my projector to watch a sick horror movie (August Underground anyone!?!) I would retrieve my nail-gun (birthday present from my wife, Stanley Electric Nail Gun £56.98 out of B&Q) and would fire a round deep into their skull. Then I would severe legs, arms and head, the heads I kept as souvenirs, the rest I put into black refuse bags and took them up to the bluebell woods known for a fact the wildlife would make a meal of them.

So now with each missing poster of each girl I wiped out on each lamp post up and down the town. With newspaper reports (which I wrote) circling all over Glasgow and the West of Scotland. A crimewatch re-enactment of the girls going missing, with no leads at all, I was becoming infamous.

And then you turn up wanting to talk to me about my stories, YOU question my involvement in the girl's disappearance and YOU think I had something to do with the girls going missing. Well obviously you are right my dear friend but I've got some bad news to tell you……YOU'RE NEXT!I hope you wiped your feet before you stepped into my house detective.

"Please don't do this Mr. Maxwell, I beg you I have kids!"

Oh stop crying you cry baby, you big cry baby does the baby want his nappy changed? Remember I have a family too.

I raised the nail-gun and fired off two rounds into the detective's skull. Within minutes he was dead, I then took my Stanley Titanium Sports Knife (Also bought by wife for my birthday out of B&Q £15.98) and began to severe through the neck and limbs. Once done I held up the detectives head, turned it and looked him in the now dead eyes.

You know detective I said I have bad news for you well the bad news my dear detective is behind every door in Drumchapel, there is a story waiting to be told.

DRUMCHAPEL

He is the devil if ever there was such a thing. The results of much too many drugs caused him to be the mind fuck that he is, completely disgusting; he didn't class himself as a human being, more of a human mutt. He was known UK wide because he was involved in murders that forensic science couldn't solve. He always felt as though he was ten feet tall with a giant set of balls.

Every thought in his mashed up mind was completely warped, with so many voices circling around in his brain, he resembled a walking talking Ouija board.   His reflection in mirrors scared him, because it wasn't him he saw but someone darker, scarier, and more evil.

He was schizoid, and he wasn't playing any jokes. So disturbed, he just goes so berserk, he slits the throats of all walking life, making them his victims his art pieces.   News broadcasts urged the public to lock their doors, if going out at night go out in pairs or groups. He resembled a whole army in one, wasn't afraid of no-one, as drugs made him invincible.

He was a psychopathic killer, a blood spiller, and certainly his mentality was much much iller, than you could imagine in your wildest dreams.

You will feel his pain as you let off a violent scream.

He simply wasn't human no more; one night while watching porn, he got his dick out and started stroking it only to feel burning pain down the whole length. He didn't catch anything from all the dead girls stored in his basement or buried in his back garden. He simply forgot that he was using a cloth smothered in lighter fluid and antifreeze. But he kept smiling; he didn't care, not in the slightest.

At first when he killed a virgin girl, he proceeded to chew on her lips, not the ones on her face but the ones between her hips. She was nineteen, sweet, angelic – he hated her. Ripped her lips off and chewed them up then spit them out. Diced her into pieces and cooked her up, ate her brains like he was Hannibal Lecter.

Psycho, slash killer like Michael Myers with a hint of Michael Jackson's Thriller. As a young one, he beaten black and blue, had his head flushed down the toilet too, but he grew stronger and grew bigger, became accustomed to a knife, a rope or hammer. Caved in skulls, women, men and girls. He was a psychopathic killer with a cheeky smile like Ben Stiller.

They say behind every door lurks a secret. If only his neighbours knew what he had hidden. Moving from town to town until he settled in a nice back and front door at the base of the bluebell woods, on a street called Summerhill. This time he wasn't planning on moving as he felt at home in Drumchapel and there were plenty of places to hide a body.

LITTLE GIRL

It was a cold January night and I was reliving my childhood. The Alien Wars show was back in Glasgow, Scotland, back in The Arches across from Glasgow Central Station. I was so looking forward to this. It was night of the ages so to speak, I first done this show back when I was eleven years old with my mum and now it was 2009 and I was twenty-nine.

I paid my fee and entered with a group of other eagerly excited people. The Alien Wars show was based on the hit movies, 'Alien' taking in the claustrophobic style of being trapped in a confided space with a thing not from our planet.

We were ushered down (into the bowels of Hell?) underground and told to stand against the wall while a man wearing a lab coat warned us and told us the back story:

'While renovating the Arches, building contractors discovered some sort of round metal disc like craft stuck deep in the foundations of the Arches. After they contacted ourselves from the Weyland Industries, we took over the excavation and what we discovered is something not from this planet'

I was hooked, so myself and the group followed the 'lab guy' and as we entered, I saw something out of the ordinary – a little girl, she must have been no more than ten years old standing there amongst the fake pipes that sprouted from the walls imitating the spaceship. She was wearing what looked like Victorian clothes; she smiled (at me?) I wasn't sure if anyone else spotted her. I turned to look at the group and then turned back to where the girl was and she was.........gone, disappeared. I stood there bewildered for about a second then I continued to follow the group.

We followed the, 'lab guy,' who finished off his story:

'We called in the Army to deal with what we discovered as we felt this was something big. Now this has never happened before well to the best of our knowledge. But the Sergeant Major has decided to grant small groups at a time to board the ship and see first-hand what a U.F.O actually looks like. So I'll hand you over to the Army.'

The, 'Lab Guy,' left and a soldier stood and told us the drill – don't do this and don't do that but do do this and do do that. The group all listened and nodded and then followed the soldier. We walked along a dark corridor and within minutes we were in a room full of egg pods, the movies let me remember that these contained, 'face huggers,' a nasty little alien that starts off the process from egg to full grown Alien, nasty nasty nasty. We walked amongst the glowing, pulsing egg pods and that's when I saw her again, the little girl stood in front of me, between myself and the group, the group obviously didn't see her – but I did! I let the group walk on so I could speak to the little girl again. I crouched down in front of her, "Hi again what's your name?"

"Amy," she told me.

"Hi Amy, I'm Jeff. Why are you here?"

"I'm hiding from the monster," she told me.

"The monster?" I began, "Oh Amy it's all special effects, it's not real and a man in a costume, a bit like you are. Where did you get those clothes from?"

"Costume?" the little girl asked puzzled, "This is my clothes." I smiled and sniggered.

"I got to hide Jeff, the monster its coming!" she sounded scared saying it, almost as if she believed in the Alien from the movies! I went to say something else but she had disappeared again.

Puzzled I got up and began quickly walking through the nest towards the group, when I heard the screech. A loud terrifying screech from behind me, from above me, from in front of me. It was all around me. It got louder and louder, and then the group I was with started screaming.

What was happening?

I ran and ran towards the group and as I turned the corner, I was met with a huge 10 foot black figure – the alien, it snarled its jaws and flexed its talons at me, I stopped in my tracks and then said, "Woah it's just you!" It snarled and snarled and swiped and swiped and then it was halved in two! The man dressed as the Alien was now in two halves, blood and guts lay strewn everywhere and there I was standing, looking up at a winged monster, taller than the movie monster, more realistic and it was lurching towards me, screeching and swiping. I ducked out of its way and ran forward towards the group………and ran and slid on the red viscus fluid – blood it was everywhere! The whole group were at the bottom of my feet dead and in bits, and the monster, the winged demon was coming towards me again. I screamed and ran down the corridor trying to find an exit, a fire exit any exit and as I neared one at the far end of the corridor, the little girl appeared again.

"No way out, Abaddon has broken free from my world, she destroyed my town and now she's going to destroy your town. It's over I'm sorry."

I screamed as the talons came ripping through my back and right through my chest. The pain was excruciating, the blood poured and I watched the very essence of my life disappear.

Abaddon destroyer of worlds had ended my life on this planet as well.

FLASHBACK

     I stayed right above James Hugh's Hairdressers on the High Street in Glasgow City Centre. I loved my wee flat; it was part of the rich history that surrounded the place – the high street in Glasgow use to be the main street of Glasgow back in the old times between the 16th century and the 19th century. I loved Glasgow, loved everything about the place.
     I awoke from a deep sleep; to a noise I wasn't familiar with – clip clop clip clop. I jumped out of bed startled and continued to hear it, it wasn't inside the flat, it was coming from outside. I didn't bother switching on a light, instead I lightened my way by my mobile phone, I entered the living room and walked over to the window, I pulled back the curtain, what I saw was something that was – well different. The High Street had changed! Instead of the new buildings that were going up I saw men, women and children in old fashioned clothes I didn't know the era but I would probably guess that it was Victorian. Was there a movie getting filmed that I didn't know about?
     Then I heard (and saw) where the constant clip clop clip clop was coming from – none other horses and carriages coming up the High Street! This was truly as though I was back in the Victorian times. I stood at the window for around ten minutes and watched this day gone by unfold in front of my very eyes. Then it was gone, the men, women and children dressed in old fashioned clothes gone. The horses and the carriages gone. The night sky was back, parked cars were back and no less than a handful of people walked the streets. I went back to my bed and climbed back in and that's when things ran through my mind:

Why didn't I record it all on my phone?

Was I dreaming?

It was weird so I updated my status on Facebook:

'Just saw the weirdest thing. Outside my window – the whole street was like back in the Victorian days then ten minutes later it changed back! I must lay off the coffee or red bull because I'm tripping now!'

I settled down and went to sleep.

The next day I had a few of my mates round for a game of Fifa on the PS4, a pizza for dinner and a few (sorry a lot) of beers. We played into the wee hours of the morning then all fell asleep. I awoke to one of my mates standing at the window in silence, just staring out of the window at something that amazed him. I got up out of the chair and walked over to him and stared out of the window too and low and behold we saw it together this time. He turned to me, "Do you see this?" I nodded but before I could actually say a word, my mate was smiling and running out of my flat, I heard him clamber down the stairs but instead of following him, I ran back to the living room window and stared out of it again as my mate emerged from the close, he stared up at me and I stared down at him. I saw people in Victorian clothes walk around him, horses and carriages going up and down the High Street. My mate stood there puzzled, I raised my arms and shrugged my shoulders saying, "What?" to him. He shook his head and stepped onto the road, he stood still puzzled as from my point of view the street began changing again back to this century, I saw the men, women and children disappear and the horses and carriages vanish, then I saw it coming fast down the road towards my mate who was totally obviously just standing there still in the middle of the road staring up at me. I banged and banged at the window, then fumbled to try and open it. My other mates woke up startled with the noise and ran to the window to stare down at our friend as the number 60 FirstBus struck him splattering him across the windshield and the road. The bus came to a sudden stop as we watched our friend's body explode literally on impact.

Police arrived shortly afterwards and questioned us, I was in two minds to tell them what I saw – what me and my now dead friend saw, but would they believe me? Or would they think I was nuts and needed help?

I chose not to say anything apart from that he was heavily intoxicated and didn't know what he was doing. I chose to keep what I saw to myself vowing never to tell anyone……until the day I was to die myself.

THE GUY WHO WENT TO THE RIVER, GAVE THE LITTLE DUCKY NONE OTHER THAN A BIT OF BREAD AND THE LITTLE DUCKY MADE HIM GET HAPPINESS

"I'm sorry Guy I got to let you go," Peter Fitzgerald of Pimms & Fitzgerald Legal Services told the man.

"Why?" Guy answered, "What have I done wrong?" Guy sat across from his boss who stared at him with folded arms across the polished oak desk. Peter sat back and let a deep breathe out then stood up. He moved over to the window that overlooked Glasgow City Centre. Ten floors up watching over the City Skyline, made Peter think he was God – Hell he had Guy's livelihood in the palm of his hands. Peter turned and looked at the quivering wreck that once was a great employee, a great lawyer, who got clients what they wanted, was able to settle things in Court and was an all-round great worker and guy. Unfortunately the past few months saw Guy become a loser so to speak unable to win cases, unable to settle out of court settlements. It just wasn't something that a company as big as Pimms & Fitzgerald wanted. They were a multimillionaire company and Guy was pulling them down into the sort of world you would get from James McGill in *Breaking Bad*! "This company Guy needs winners and I'm sorry to say this but you're a loser plain and simple," Peter continued, "You have by the end of the day to clear out your office, you're fired."

"End of the day?" Guy began raising his voice, "End of the BLOODY DAY! Screw you Peter! Screw you, I'll leave the now." Guy stood up and began walking towards the door to his boss's office and then he turned back, with tears in his eyes, "I gave my life to this company, overtime, working long nights away from my wife and kids and for the last few months yeah I've had a poor time but to fire me? To let me go? As you put it! Well fuck you Peter, fuck you and I hope you die a horrible horrible death, I hope you slip and fall from a great height and bash you brains in and when that eventually happens I am going to be drinking champagne and dancing the Macarena. So here's my parting gift to you Peter my dear friend I call this my, 'kiss my arse,' salute!" Guy kissed his hand placed it on his behind and then gave his ex-boss a two fingered salute.

Peter picked up the telephone and dialed security to come and escort Guy out of the building. They allowed him to grab his things from his office and then forcefully removed him from the building.

Guy sat on the wall outside the building looking up to the top of the building. He then gave the same two fingered salute to the building, picked up his box full of personal items and headed down the road to the nearest pub. He drank and drank until very late on in the night; he checked his phone constantly to see if there were any missed calls or texts from his wife but absolutely nothing. He did understand though, Nancy knew he hated being disturbed at work so never called him; she just waited for him to call her. Feeling really tipsy, Guy called a taxi and headed home it was around 8pm. He paid the driver and exited the cab; he staggered up the driveway – puking up over Nancy's lovely roses that were now in full bloom. He laughed hard and then made a mental note:

'Get fresh roses and plant them in garden'

He fought with the key in the keyhole before opening the front door and stumbling through into the living room. All was silent, which was very unusual as Nancy's care was in the driveway. Puzzled he began climbing the stairs, when he reached the top he heard noises. Not normal noises but noises like moaning – sexual moaning noises. Within a matter of seconds Guy was sober as he barged into the marital bedroom and with his own eyes there in front of him bouncing up and down, writhing about on the bed was his wife fully naked with a man underneath her. He saw everything!

"What the fuck?" Guy screamed.

Nancy startled jumped off her lover and stood fully naked in front of her husband. Her lover sat there with his face partially covered by the quilt cover.

"Okay Guy," Nancy began, "Calm down start breathing......." "START BREATHING!" Guy yelled, "I just caught you cheating!"

Nancy reached for her dressing gown and pulled it round her, "It's not what it seems."

"What you tripped; fell, landed on his dick!" Guy yelled. "What a fucking thing to say Nancy! Really – it's not what it looks like. You are nothing but a whore!"

"Hey, hey, hey," came the man's voice from the bed, "don't call her that!"

Guy knew the voice, hell he knew the man that was shagging his wife, "Peter you fucking prick!" He ran round the side of the bed to grab hold of his ex-boss. Peter jumped out the other side, bullock naked and ran out the room and down the stairs grabbing his trousers in the process. Guy ran after him and watched as he made a beeline out the front door. Guy threw Peter's shirt, jacket and shoes at him, "I hope you die you cheating backstabbing fucking bastard!" He then went back in the house and marched up the stairs, by this time Nancy had started packing up her clothes into a suitcase.

"Where are you going?" Guy asked.

"It's over Guy it's been over for so long," Nancy began, "You just don't satisfy me anymore, I need a man, a man that can touch me in the right places, a man that can be here with me instead of working late. So I'm leaving you and I'm taking the kids. I'm moving in with Peter and I want a divorce."

Tears began forming in his eyes, "I was working late to keep you........." Guy stopped and thought about the past few months, him working late, Peter finishing early or on time. "Peter was coming round here and fucking you while I was slaving over a job I was about to lose wasn't he? Peter has been screwing you for months now hasn't he? Where are the kids anyway Nancy?"

Nancy nodded at the first questions then added, "Peter's sister is babysitting them."

"Well whoop-tae-do," Guy yelled, "happy families I see then? You know what get out, get out now and don't bother coming back and yeah your divorce you got it, but you aren't getting a penny from me whatsoever so don't bother asking!"

"I don't want anything from you," Nancy replied. She picked up the suitcase and walked down the stairs. Guy followed making sure she left the house. As she walked down the driveway he called, "Hey Nancy I hope to God you get hit by a number 60 bus or even better catch fucking crabs from good old jolly Pervy Pete. You know he fucks all his personal assistants don't you? Fucks them over his desk. Who knows what diseases he has? Enjoy!" With that said he slammed the door shut. He walked back into the living room and slouched on the couch and began crying.

Later that night he took to watching porn on the TV while playing slots online, he deposited from their joint bank account a £1000 at a time and was spinning the reels at £100 a time. He never did anything back. Within three hours, the joint bank account was emptied, no savings no nothing. He smiled and drank direct from his bottle of rum and then laughed. In a mere twelve hours, he had lost his job, lost his wife and kids and sure to God will end up losing his house (the mortgage was to come out first thing tomorrow from the bank account and after three months of defaults it was a certain that the bank would repose the house.) He laughed uncontrollably before falling into a deep sleep.

The following day, he awoke with an almighty hangover and to at least ten missed calls from the bank. When they called again he told them to go fuck themselves and take the heap of trash that is the house back because he wasn't going be here anymore. He had made his mind up – he was going to kill himself. He opened up the cupboard in the hall and pulled out his rucksack, he went out into the garden and from the rockery he began piling stones into the bag to make it extremely heavy. He placed the bag in his car and then grabbed a loaf of bread, some meat (last supper so to speak.) He then got in his car and drove down to the River Clyde. He parked his car in a secluded area and threw the heavy rucksack over his shoulder and headed down to the Clyde side. As he stared out across the river, his life flashed before his eyes. His ups and downs and he knew today was the day that he was ending it all. Then he heard it a small squeaky noise, constant squeaky noise. He looked around until he noticed that the noise was coming from some big reeds at the side of the river. He carried his rucksack over to the noise and placed it on the ground, he then explored the long reeds by pulling them apart only to a little duck, stuck in amongst the reeds. He looked about but so no mother or father of the little duck.

"Hi little ducky," Guy said smiling, "Are you lost and stuck?" He laughed to himself, here he was contemplating suicide and now he was sitting talking to a little duck! "Do you want some bread? I have bread and meat here. It was going to be my last thing I ate but I can share with you."

He tried to reach in to remove the trapped animal, but couldn't quite reach so he decided to coax it out. He opened up his rucksack and pulled the meat and bread out. He began tearing the bread into small pieces and threw them into the water. The little duck quacked and quacked then began moving out of the reeds. The little thing began eating the bread furiously.

"Jeezo you must have been starving!" Guy smiled, "eat up little ducky, eat up."

In that split second of watching (and helping) the little duck, Guy felt good inside. The little duck looked up at him and swam in circles before letting off a high pitched quack and swimming up the River Clyde. Guy smiled and shouted, "See you later little ducky, take care!" he still felt stupid saying it but inside him, for some reason he felt good about and decided not to kill himself.

He emptied the rucksack of the stones and stood up; he looked across the water and said aloud, "Please, please let my luck change. Let me be my own boss, have a mansion with an indoor pool, have a very hot girlfriend. Make me be a millionaire."

He could only dream......

He fell asleep in the car and awoke to the sound of his phone ringing away to the tune of *Eminem's Lose Yourself*. He sat up straight grabbed his phone off the dashboard and looked at who was calling it read:

PIMMS & DAPPY

Puzzled at first as to why someone would change the name of his old company in his phone to Pimms and his surname, he answered it.

"Hello?" Guy answered.

"Hello sir. It's Becky. Mr. Pimms is asking where you are. You were supposed to meet him for drinks then a round of golf and he's been waiting for over an hour!"

"Becky?" Guy questioned still puzzled.

"Yes sir?" Becky responded.

"Why is it in my phone as PIMMS & DAPPY?" Guy asked.

"What sir?" Becky laughed, "See this is why I love you outside work and like being your personal assistant in work you make me laugh. You took over from Peter Fitzgerald after he committed embezzlement to the highest degree then threw himself out of his office window ten floors up. Sad, sad day sir but to be honest you turned this company round, you made the company worth millions and a great place to work."

"When did I take over Becky and sorry to say this when

did we start seeing each other? I thought I was married!" Guy asked bewildered.

"Sir you took over three months ago and we started seeing each other after your wife passed away. I was there for you as a shoulder to cry on and the rest they say is history. I'm shocked you can't remember and a bit angry but I know why you can't remember – you were on the rum last night weren't you?" Becky laughed.

"I……yes now that I recall I was on the rum," Guy answered.

"I told you not to drink that stuff it always makes you forgot honey. But no worries I still love you more than anything. Anyway before I forgot my mum is taking the kids tonight so we can have some alone time and I was thinking about the toys you bought me from Pabo.com, if you want to use them on me tonight?"

Guy smiled a whole new life.
What the hell had happened?
Did God answer his demands?
Did God actual exist and listen to him?

"That sounds wonderful Becky, in fact sounds like a real good plan," Guy replied.

"Well I'll come by the golf course around 7pm that gives you and Mr. Pimms time to finish your boy stuff together, oh and I took out £3000 from the account hope you don't mind, I wanted to buy you that state of the art Sony Blu-ray projector and all those horror movies. Oh and I bought you the PlayStation 4 so that'll go nicely in the games room that means we have all the consoles from the original Atari to the PlayStation 4. I can't wait to beat your ass at C.O.D!" Becky told him, "Anyway get over to Dalmuir Golf Course before Pimms decides to send you away to Dubai again, which means no more boom-boom in the room-room for a while! Love you Guy see you soon."   Guy hung up the phone then sat puzzled but excited, feeling strange but happy. He opened up his phone and clicked on the gallery to view pictures. He saw himself and a beautiful brunette long curvaceous woman by his estimate around 23 years old, him being 31 years old he felt happy about. He sat for a few minutes more pondering what had happened to his wife how did she die? So he done the naturally thing and typed into Google:

NANCY DAPPY DEAD

A news article came up from the Daily Record tabloid paper it read:

On the morning of May 15th Nancy Dappy stepped out in front of a number 60 FirstBus causing the bus to collide with her. Mrs. Dappy died on impact. She leaves behind a widower Guy Dappy and two young children. Mr. Dappy gave us what he believed to be a suicide note written by Mrs. Dappy it read: 'Guy I am sorry for what I did with Peter I ruined you, the company and the kids. I miss Peter so now I want to be with him. Goodbye – Nancy' Mr. Dappy laid his wife to rest and now takes full care of their children.

He actually laughed at the news article. Did he dream about this? He remembers leaving his boss Peter of Pimms & Fitzgerald's office telling him he hoped he died by falling from a great height – he did he threw himself out the window! He also remembered he told his cheating wife that he hoped she got hit by a bus – she did. And now here he was sitting in his……….Lotus car!?! Hold on Lotus car!?! He opened up his banking app on his phone and checked his bank balance it read £15,577,493.97. He was a frigging millionaire! He punched into the GPS system Dalmuir Golf Course and sped off away from the River Clyde, heading for his drinks and round of golf with his business partner.

As he stepped out the car, he saw his business partner (old boss) Jeff Pimms standing at a table in the beer garden outside. He walked over to him.

"What kept you buddy?" Pimms asked, "Were you fucking that nice piece of ass you have as a bird again?"

Guy shook hands and replied smiling, "Not today Jeff I was actually just sitting down at the River Clyde feeding this little ducky that got caught in some long reeds and I……totally forgot about the time and what I was doing!" he lied but it fitted in well with what was happening in this surreal sort of world.

"See Guy that's why you are a top notch man, a decent human being and an all-round great friend. You care about stuff and now look at us millionaires, the company is making thousands per day, you have Becky and I have well anyone I choose to have on a daily basis!" Pimms responded slapping Guy on the shoulder. They both laughed, drunk more scotch than they could manage and down a great wee round of golf where Guy won.

Guy's life had turned around dramatically and he loved every part of it. When Becky turned up in her Mercedes to drive both Pimms and her man back home. She dropped Pimms off first then continued home with Guy. Guy askedher if they could stop off at the River Clyde where he was parked earlier today. Becky did just that and Guy walked down to the river bed. In the distance he saw a group of ducklings along with their parents all swimming down the water. He heard them quacking away and smiled; just then one of the ducklings came out of the group of siblings and swam fast over to Guy. Guy smiled as soon as he saw the cute little ducky swimming towards him.

"Hi little ducky," Guy began, "Did you cause all this? Did you change my life around?"

The little duck just quacked loudly before swimming back to his brothers and sisters.

Guy stood up and smiled; if it was indeed the little duck then he thanked him for everything. He walked away back up to his girlfriend and they both drove away back to their mansion in Cardross.

NO EXIT

No way out. No way out. I was stuck.
No escape. No escape. I was trapped.
I turned and turned around looking for a way to get out. Twisting down the corridors. Turning round each corner going nowhere.
Why me?
Why did he pick me for his cruel game?
What did I ever do to deserve this?
I could hear him laugh. No wait cackle, yes cackle.
"Nowhere to run, nowhere to hide. I will get you my pretty and I will gut you."
I began running fast down the corridor. Doors passed by me, doors that didn't open. Gave me no help whatsoever.
"I'm coming to get you!" he cackled again. "You can't escape so why try? Just stop and wait till I get a hold of you. It would be better for you in the long run." I wasn't giving in, I continued running then I saw it the bright green neon sign:

EXIT

Yes, yes, YES! I had made it. I ran to the door and pushed with all my strength on the door bar. The door creaked and opened fully. I walked through the exit door and out into........A boiler room.
The heat was intense. The steam poured from the pipes. He was right after all there was no escape there was no exit. Then I heard the door open and there standing in the door was the man. My tormentor. The man that wouldn't let me go.
I had nowhere to hide. I stood there glued to the spot in front of him as he marched up to me.
"I got you!" he declared.
I looked at him, tears forming in my eyes. "What do you want from me?"

"To be free. Free from your memory. It's not your fault you can't remember what you did but I'm willing to show and make you remember."

He placed a hand on the top of my head. I closed my eyes and everything went black and then I saw it, I was kneeling down on the ground with my arms outstretched, "Die, die, DIE!" I was screaming. Then I saw what I was doing. There below me turning a nice shade of blue.......Was my father.

I killed my father and suppressed the memory.

There was simply no exit from what I did.

HAVE YOUR CAKE AND EAT IT

For years on end it's been a tradition in my household to buy a Halloween cake and celebrate the week before Halloween by watching horror movies and eating sweets and scoffing cake by the handful.

This year, for some reason it all changed. My family didn't want to do that anymore. I felt sad, I mean this was a tradition, this was Halloween and we always did this sort of thing and I wasn't going to change it.

Okay so my family didn't buy any cake in or sweets in, Hell they even switched off the movie channels on SKY so no horror for the household at all, DVDS and Blurays were banned. This Halloween was going to be crap. Even costumes were prohibited.

But you know what, I WAS going to celebrate Halloween like I always did and no one was going to spoil it for me - in fact I was going to spoil theirs.

First up was my costume - the infamous and badass Michael Myers. I donned the mask (Halloween 4's mask which is way scarier than the original mask.) I stood in the shadows in our garden watching and waiting for my family to appear. First up was my dear old mum, as she walked up the footpath to the front door I stepped up behind her, breathing hard and fast I raised the kitchen knife and disposed of her by running the knife along her throat, blood pumped hard and fast as she spun round and screamed.

Don't worry it was a fake knife that squirted blood. Do you honestly think I was going to slit my mother's own throat? Hey I'm not that sick.

"Billy," she yelled, "I told you no more Halloween in our house why can't you understand that? Now take off the costume and get back inside."

So I did. But I wasn't finished.

My dad was next, I was standing in the kitchen running

my hand over various kitchen knives and meat tenderisers when he entered and walked over to the fridge to retrieve his daily Budweiser.

"Hey dad watch this!" I called to him.

He turned and watched as I brought the meat tenderiser down onto my right hand shattering it into tiny pieces, he screamed blue murder raced over to me and pulled the mallet off of me, when I laughed uncontrollably, I pulled the rubber hand out of my sleeve which was filled with red food colouring minced meat.

"Billy!" he yelled at me, "You little shit get out of my face, you nearly gave me a heart attack! Go to your room now!"

I couldn't stop laughing but did what my dad said. I trudged up the stairs and into my room. I sat on my bed and fired up the PlayStation 4 putting on, 'Until Dawn,' a bloody scary slasher game.

About an hour or so later both my parents shouted on me, "Billy come down here we have a little surprise for you."

I smiled, paused the game and ran out my bedroom and down the stairs.

"Billy," my mum began, "Here I made a Halloween cake for you come and have a bit."

I sat down on the couch and my mum handed me a huge thick slice of chocolate covered jammed filled Halloween cake. I picked it up and shoveled it into my mouth. Chopping and munching it down until I felt a weird burning sensation in my throat. I raised my left hand to my throat and felt a lump of some sort and it moved under my fingers. I pulled my hand away and there was blood on my fingertips. I looked up at my mum and dad and they just sat there and smiled at me as I shot up and raced to the mirror hanging over the fireplace. I raised my head so I could look at my neck and prodded at the lump that protruded from my throat with my fingers again and then I felt it pierce through my skin, I pulled at it and pulled at it as it began to tear my throat apart. Blood poured down my neck as I retrieved what was the lump in my throat - it was none other than a razor blade!

I turned and looked at my parents before collapsing in a heap in front of them. "Who's fucked now Billy!" my mum laughed.

"Happy fucking Halloween jackass!" My dad chimed in.

Maybe I should have listened to my family when they said no more Halloween.

The last thing I saw was my parents laugh at me as I ebbed deep into the darkness of the abyss of death.

SLEEP, THOSE LITTLE SLICES OF DEATH

I've had at least five hours sleep over the course of the past three days. It has made me angry and moody (there is no doubt about it.)

Sleep deprived and not fully focused.

But I've been seeing things, hearing things. I can't describe exactly what these things are except that it's a dark shadow almost like a blob. Every time I blink I see strange lights.

Oh God here it comes again.....the headache, it, it's powerful as if the whole world is on top of my head. Pressing down forcing my neck to collapse. Oh the pain it's excruciating.

Then there are the colours, the dancing blues and greens in front of my eyes. The pain it causes, I, I can't focus it's too sore to focus.

Pain, suffering, anger and sleep deprivation. I claw at my eyes, wanting to pluck my eyes out. Wanting to stop the pain. I bang my fists against my temples causing more pain. Yip it doesn't take it away.

I really don't know what to do.

Do I try and sleep?

What happens if I don't wake up?

Oh the pain is back its tearing at my forehead at my eye sockets.

Got to sleep, got to sleep for a while.

Maybe this straight razor blade will ease the pain in my head!

I hold it between my thumb and fore finger and hold it to the side of my forehead and gradually pull it along. A thin trickle of blood flows from a small straight lined cut. I breathe deeply. But the pain and the stress of not sleeping are still there. Blood flows slowly from my open wound as I blink again seeing the blues and greens. It's making me sick. I need it to stop, stop now. STOP NOW FOR GOD SAKE!

    I stare at the straight razor and raise it to my left eye and begin cutting into my eye, eye juice and blood begins to pour then a small, 'pop,' noise as my eye deflates and I can't see out of it. I do the same to my right eye and now seeing nothing.　　　　No blues no greens. Just darkness. I am in peace for all of five minutes until my head pounds in pain again.

    I scream ARGHHHHHHHHH before throwing myself forward and into the glass bathroom cabinet. Glass pierces my skin over my face and I feel the blood pour down the side of my neck. I have hit the artery.

    Within minutes I have collapsed onto the bathroom floor.

    I am sleeping now.

ON THE MENU

Have you ever dabbled in eating human beings?

A simple slice of thigh meat looks like carver ham if cut thin.

A slice of calf (left or right) tastes like pork. But you have to fry it in sunflower oil and add some seasoning - I prefer using just plain old salt and pepper.   The meat off of the fingers is a bit like pulled pork. (Not KFC certified!)

It all started a few years back when my pet dog was turned into a pancake by a BP Oil Tanker. The bastard driver didn't even stop. So I retrieved a black refuse sack and scoped Snowy up and placed him in the bag. I went home and told my parents only for them to say, 'You bury your own!' So I went outside, dug a hole big enough for my Labrador. But when I was ready to place Snowy into the make-shift grave, I reached in and touched the flesh that clung to the bone. I removed my hand and it was covered in blood, I examined it for a bit then raised it to my mouth and licked the blood clean off my hand.

It tasted nice.

From behind me I heard my parents shout, 'That's us off now Ryan. Money on the table for a takeaway for you. We won't be back till late, now don't stay up to late playing that damn Resident Evil game.' I waved them away and as I watched them leave. Something triggered in my head, it was like a little voice telling me something.   'Eat the dog. Go on taste it. You know you want to.'

I nodded (too who I don't know!) I turned and headed back into the house with my dead pooch. I entered the kitchen. Started up the cooker and placed the dead dog on the centre counter. I retrieved various knives, I then got my electric razor and began shaving off all the hair before cutting into the flesh, cutting strips of the dog meat into layers some small some large. I got the baking tray and placed the various parts onto the tray and then placed it in the oven for around thirty minutes.

I sat down later on and enjoyed the dog meat burger with cheese.

That was then, now I have graduated to humans. Not any humans, the humans have to be disease free.

'I ate his liver with some fava beans and a nice bottle of chianti'

I love that line from Silence of the Lambs!

Anyway I didn't just carve out his liver, I took out his kidneys, his heart and also I ate part of his brain.

'More brains!'

Ha! Tar man from Return of the living dead always makes me laugh. So now after all these years I have eaten or partially eaten about fifty humans. Men, women and children (in between a few more cats and dogs oh and a snake!) The snake was like a nice Richmond Pork sausage.

I live by myself and my neighbours don't suspect a thing. The way I capture my dinner is simply by following them or even if I see a nice person in a bar. I slip them some sleeping tablets and BOOM! That's me got my meal for the night. So I'm just warning you, if a guy offers you a drink in a pub or night club or if you think someone is following. Be on your guard because it could well be me.

THE BUS RIDE

There they were laughing and joking about me. Me a nice guy. Kind. Charming. Pleasant. A loner. I keep myself to myself and that is what seems to be the problem with people. The stare at me all the time on the bus. Laughing. Joking. Pointing at me but today is the day that I laugh at them. Today I make a statement. They got up to get off the bus by pressing the button. It was only myself, them two and the driver on the last bus of the night. But the driver continued driving.

"Hey driver that was our stop!" said one of the girls.

The driver didn't listen and pit his foot down, flooring the bus to full speed. I gripped on to the seat in front of me. I was scared too.

"Driver please stop!" exclaimed the other girl becoming terrified.

Still the driver didn't listen, didn't respond.

Then we went off road, up a dirt road leading to the woods. The bus bounced and bashed across the pot-holed road then came to a full stop in the middle of the woods. The driver turned off the ignition and opened the door. He got up and walked off the bus. He walked over to a tree stump and sat down, pulling out a carton of cigarettes and proceeded to light one up.

I stared out at him through the window, I just wasn't expecting this. Not when I was going to humiliate the girls and laugh and point at them. I guess that just has to wait till another day. I stared back at the girls, who cuddled each other they were certainly terrified. I stood up and walked passed them and exited the bus. I turned to them, extended my hand, "Come on let's go!"

The first girl took my hand and I guided her off then the other girl followed. I looked at the driver but he didn't move, didn't flinch. He just sat there.

"Go," I told the girls, "RUN!"

They didn't need told twice. They both turned and were just about to run, when I produced the hammer concealed in my inside jacket pocket and walked the second girl over the head once, twice, three times before she fell to the ground and bone and head meat spilled to the ground. The other girl turned and was about to scream when I raised the claw hammer, spun it round and with sheer force I swung the claw end and it stuck deep into her forehead. Breaking the skull and piercing the brain below. Blood pooled before she also feel to the ground.

I pulled the hammer out of the skull, stood tall then I laughed uncontrollably while pointing at them.

I turned to the driver who got up from the tree stump and began walking over to me quickly. "Right son let's get home, mums got dinner on."

"What we having?" I asked while getting back on the bus.

"Minced meat and chips," my dad said.

I laughed hysterically as my dad started up the engine and we made our way home.

THE MONSTER

When I was about twelve years old, I came down with a really bad case of the flu virus. I lived with my mum and my big brother in a first floor tenement flat in Dunkenny Road Drumchapel. The sweats, the coughs, the sniffles annoyed me but thankfully I had my mum, my soul mate to look after and take care of me.

It was on a cold winter night when it came for me and my family. I fell asleep on the sofa with my head in my mums lap. My mum waited about an hour before lifting me up and carrying me into my bedroom. She tucked me in and gave me a kiss goodnight on my forehead as she always did.

A little into my peaceful (so to speak) slumber, I awoke with such a fright. I stared over at my big brothers bed, peering through the shadows, through my teenage mutant ninja turtle figures and my brothers Glasgow Rangers posters and one of pop star Kylie Minogue. I heard it, the scratching, as if it was nails getting scratched down a blackboard. I lay there in fear at first and called to my brother.

"Scott! Scott! Scott did you hear that?"

No response came from his bed; I peered again through the shadows and noticed that my brother wasn't in his bed.

Where was he?

I threw back the covers and ran to the bedroom door, I ran out into the hallway and up into the living room. There I saw my mum sitting on the couch.

"Mum! Mum! Scott's………Scott's not in his bed, I heard scratching and screeching noises and Scott's not in his bed!"

I trembled all over, sweat poured off me, I was literally swimming in a pool of my own sweat. I ran over to my mum and she embraced me with a warm hug.

"David," she began soothing me, "Scott's over there lying in front of the TV. You jumped over him silly!"

She turned me round and I focused my eyes on the front of the TV. But there was no Scott there. There was no big brother. Then the screeching and scratching came again. On the TV screen weird looking brown coloured monsters were lurching after someone – coming directly towards the TV screen. I freaked out and turned to my mum, "Where? I don't see him! He's gone."

"David he's there can't you see him honey?" my mum reassured me.

I shook my head, tears running down my face. Then the screeching and scratching started again then came the voice......

"David, I have them all!"

I looked about, looking for the voice but saw no body, nothing from where the voice was coming from.

"David, up here!" the voice boomed down at me.

I lifted my head towards the living room ceiling and saw the hideous monster with knives for fingers and razors sticking out of its back. I glanced along the ceiling and there I saw my dad gutted and halved in two. My big brother Scott lying at the monsters feet, his intestines wrapped around the ceiling light swinging back and forth. Then there was the other body......the monster held my mother by the throat! My mother I turned towards the sofa and yes my mum was gone! She was now up on the ceiling and I watched her getting her head cut off by the monster.

I screamed and screamed as the blood of my family splashed and dripped onto me I was covered in the rich red water.

Then I jumped up out of my mother's lap after she screamed about a dozen times at me to waken up.

I sat bolt upright and stared right up at the ceiling – a clean white painted ceiling, no monsters, no bodies, no blood. I stared about the living room and there sprawled out in front of the TV, as white as a ghost staring at me, tears rolling down his cheeks was my big brother Scott. Scared for me.

I had a nightmare that night. It felt so real and I felt as though I lost my whole family. Blame it on the flu virus, on something I watched on the TV or simply on a vivid imagination. But I didn't want to lose my family when I was twelve and certainly don't want to lose them now.

MY WAY

Ah the uncleansed disease of our Country. They believe they are special, they do. I can see it in their eyes.

In this society if you're a junkie you literally get what you want. But I vowed that I would fight, fight to clear the disease from our streets. It's not about just cleaning up the streets of the filth, but about leadership. Once it's done and dusted, I will then straight up leave this crap because I've had enough of this, I am simply pissed.

I am of course talking about the drug addicts, the heroin abusers or as us Scots call them – junkies. I had enough of my hard earned money going towards junkies, who were constantly getting handouts from the Government and the Social, whether it be on benefits (if you have a needle in your arm – here there's a house rent free and here's £400 a month to keep you.) Or even the methadone program. As far as I was concerned they got in this mess, so let them rot!

It all really came to a head when one of the uncleansed asked me for, 'some spare change for a cup of tea,' I asked them if they were homeless. 'No,' came the reply. So why was he asking me for spare change?

Surely only homeless people ask that question?

It turned out he needed a fix and as he didn't go for his medical. His money was sanctioned for 4 weeks.

Four bloody weeks! He hasn't got money to live on for a month, a bit like me because I don't get paid for another month, but hey I manage and so should he. I turned to him and said, "Get a job you junkie bastard. What did you think I was just going to open my wallet and give you money? Get the Hell out of my face, go a crawl under the rock you came out from!"

I walked away down the road, turned down the alleyway which I use for a shortcut home and then I heard walking behind me. I turned to see – El Jako standing scratching his disease ridden face, and through his rotten teeth in his mouth he spoke the words which to tell you the truth I knew was coming.

"Geez yer wallet!" he produced a needle. Probably a dirty one at that and began advancing towards me.

I smirked, "seriously, 'geez yer wallet,' you're really going to use those words while coming at me with a needle? Get to fuck you wee rat!"

"Just geez it noo!" the toothless aggression came out from him. Oh those rotten yellow and black teeth. If I just had a set of pliers……

"Listen dick, one word – no!" I began then I changed my mind – to an extent. I pulled out my wallet, opened it up and pulled out the £500 of notes I just took out for my rent and council tax. I waved it at him, "You want this? Come and get it!"

I didn't have to tell the sewer dweller twice, he rushed at me with the needle out far in his right hand and went to grab the cash, when I spun him around, tripped him up and he landed hard amongst the trash and black bin bags, he screamed in pain as I watched from above him. You see his dirty needle well it was stuck in his neck!

I bent down and plunged the actual plunger which just contained air (and probably a few other stuff!) into his neck. I then snapped the syringe off leaving the needle deep in his neck. He thrashed about and within thirty seconds he was dead. I stood up and left him there and walked out of the alley when I heard scratching and scurrying behind me. I pulled out my mobile phone, turned on the torch and flashed it over the area behind me and that's when I saw them. There crawling all over the junkies body were rats, big black disgusting filthy rats eating the junkie.

Rats eating a rat – ironic that isn't is!

GOD/DEVIL: THE EARTH IS THEIR PLAYING FIELD

As of the end of 2014, 85 per cent of the world's population believed in a God (the apparent creator of earth and humans) this is down by 11 per cent since 2011.

Of the population of the whole world, 850 million people believe in not God but only his brother - the Devil as we know him by.

With so much death and destruction in the world and not a lot of 'miracles' or people turning water to wine. Then it's only necessary to believe in the dark lord of hell, rather than his timid (and less seen brother up in the sky)

I believe in the devil and I've met him on so many different times of my life.

He told me various things like, 'us humans are puppets,' born to this planet to do the evil that men do. To strike fear in every walks of life and to scare the fact that god, 'upstairs,' doesn't give a flying fuck!

Lucifer spoke to me one night as I lay in my bed-sit, he told me that I had to do the, 'right thing,' show the world that its playtime for him and hopefully his dear brother will get his fat lazy arse off the clouds and come down and face his dear old brother rather than let him watch as, he puts it, 'his creation of man destroying one and other.'

I was to be the soldier of Lucifer, was to do something so diabolical that I will be noticed worldwide.

It took me a few days to think of the perfect thing to do to get God off his cloud recliner and down here to fight his brother. Then I came up with the ideal solution, a big ass lock down in a shopping centre.

I knew that thousands passed through the doors of Buchanan Galleries in Glasgow city centre, day in and day out, every single day of the week.

Now I had to secure all exits and emergency exits and make sure it was on total lock down.

Best way to do that - well that's simple, I phoned the security informed them that there are various bombs around the building and multi-storey car park. And if anyone was to leave the building then BOOM the building will go up in smoke. I told them to lock all doors and keep everyone on the ground floor and don't let anyone in. One brave little soldier (a pumped up security guard that looked like a pit-bull dog, I nicknamed 'Spike,' well he dared me to prove that there was bombs about the building.

Well let's just say, they are picking up pieces of him on the main escalators as his body was blown apart by a homemade bomb containing nails and glass.

Bye-bye Spike.

So now they knew I wasn't joking. So all exits, emergency doors and car park entrances got all secured shut.

The police were called in, along with the bomb squad and a someone to bargain with me. (As if I was going to do a deal. I'm doing the Devils work for fuck sake!)

So they ask me why I was doing this. I told them that it was for a, 'bigger picture,' which needless to say they didn't understand!

I told them that every 10 minutes; a bomb will go off killing a group of trapped, filthy humans until they understood the reason behind this.

I heard screams of, 'oh god,' and, 'for the love of Christ please stop!'

I responded, 'Where is your saviour now?' Needless to say they just cried, and then BOOM another bomb went off, this one was a bit special, it contained the same as the previous (Spike) bomb. But I added a nerve gas.

For the trapped filthy humans near the bomb, they received severed limbs and deep cuts to the body, but the nerve gas entered their blood stream and within moments their insides became their outsides!

At least 20 were confirmed dead, gone, away from this planet. Still no god, however the devil stood next to me admiring the work in front of him, admiring how many souls he had now collected.

But still no saviour and creator of the world.

This I called, 'the worlds end murders,' due to the fact, this was being televised around the world.

Police asked me again to stop and guess what - I said no and BOOM I brought the top floor to come crashing down on the stricken humans that infested the building.

Confirmed dead - 400.

Lucifer wanted me to go out on a high but said to me if I did what he wanted, then he will grant me immortality.

To live forever, without getting old.

I agreed, he ordered me to strap a nail/glass bomb onto me combined with the TNT around my waist and I was to enter the building and run right into the remaining filthy humans and detonate the bomb causing mass destruction.

I agreed - hell for immortality I would cut my own wrists and drink my blood!

So strapped up, I entered the building, through my secret door (it was actually a vent shaft leading outside.)

I saw the rest of the group and ran right up to them and as they parted I press the button and BOOM blew the rest of the group and myself and the remaining building up into smithereens.

I left my body, my soul climbed out and that's when I saw the escalators, one going up and one going down. With a sign saying:

YOUR CHOICE

I of course wanted to see what the up escalator took me too. But unfortunately as I neared it - it vanished all that was left was the down escalator.

I heard a snigger from behind me and I turned around, there standing behind me was none other than Lucifer.

"Did you honestly think that if you did what I asked, I would give you immortality? I'm the fucking devil, the greatest practical joker the world has ever seen!"

"But where do I go now?" I asked.

"I don't give a fuck. I got what I wanted!" He told me. And with that, he vanished.

The escalators were gone and the place became dark, so dark I couldn't see anything.

This was my life now, a life of sin. A life of purgatory.

Forgive me father for I have sinned.

End.

ALSO FROM D P SLOAN

GO TO SLEEP

Drugs Don't Work
19th January 2000

Sweating came on him extremely badly; he wanted his next fix as soon as possible. He had become addicted to all sorts of drugs; he tried going cold turkey, but only lasted two hours. More hatred for his mother and father poured from every hole in his body. His dear old daddy left him and Andrew with this thing that they called a mother. Now he was away from the hell house, but the craving for drugs just got more and more intense. He already got his jobseeker's money but that all went on electricity and food - all of twenty pounds worth, mostly made up of microwave meals, ten pence crisps and Irn Bru. The rest of his money went on drugs: cocaine, hash, blues you name it – anything he could get. He had spent all his money by 11 a.m. Now he was feeling the effects, he needed something almost for the pain as such. But with no money the next best thing was...to steal.

He walked down the pavement on his way to the local shopping centre, an old woman pulling her shopping trolley passed by him and looked at him with disgust. He snarled at her. "What you looking at you old bitch?" With shock and awe she tsk-tsk him and carried on walking. Or, as he thought, waddled down passed him. He was angrier now, how dare she stare at him as though he was a piece of shit? He turned on his heels and started following her; slowly behind her so she wouldn't suspect a thing. She was totally oblivious to him following her. She continued on her journey home (he gathered) - she turned left and walked down a lane, which was littered with garbage. (Hell what do you expect – you are in Clydebank after all!) He picked up his pace and on closing in on the old bitch, he pulled a small stainless steel serrated knife out of his pocket. (It was to threaten staff at the shops for when he was going to steal from them.) He got closer and closer and just as he neared her, she turned to face him – eyes wide with fright.

"Remember me!" he growled at her.

The old woman didn't say a word just stood there, shaking.

"You fucking old cunt you stared at me – you got a problem with me? The way I look? Fucking talk to me bitch!" he yelled at her, not too loud for people to hear.

"I'm...I'm sorry," the old woman stammered.

He just smiled at her. "Well I'm not!" He showed her the knife, and with such force he plunged it deep into her stomach two, maybe three times. When he pulled the blade out, the old woman tried to cower and cover her wounds but that didn't help her, and with rage in his eyes, he forced the knife again, but this time in to her sides and then started swiping the blade in slashing motion all over her arms. Then as she fell to the ground, surrounded by garbage, he raised the knife and plunged it deep into her left eye, but not too deep as that would have pierced her brain. He heard a *pop* noise as her eye juices flowed from her socket, and as he pulled the knife out he heard a voice saying, 'finish her!' - And he did just that. He raised the knife one last time and aimed it directly between her sagging breasts and forced it through her chest cavity directly into her heart.

He stood up and glanced down, but with no remorse he bent down grabbed the now blood covered dead woman's purse from her jacket pocket and then walked away, while checking the purse. "Jackpot!" he said to himself. "She must have just cashed out her pension." In the purse was four hundred pounds - he walked away a happy man.

First murder – drug dependency.

AVAILABLE FROM Spinetinglers, Amazon, Waterstones, Barnes & Noble, WH Smith in paperback and available on Kindle from Amazon kindle store. Buy your copy from D P Sloan himself and get it autographed for more info contact D P Sloan at videonasties@sky.com

COMING WINTER 2016 THE NEXT PART IN THE GO TO SLEEP SERIES

D P SLOAN'S

GO TO SLEEP 3

He took his time slitting the old woman's throat; he was going to show Dalmuir that the ripper is not someone you should mess with. As for that James Maxwell and his book, 'Light of Darkness,' he was using that as a step-by-step guide in killing. First up was the old woman who stared at him the wrong way. With a knife in hand he stabbed her thirteen times in the chest, before slitting her throat. In the dead of the night he carried her up the hill of Dalmuir Park and displayed her on the grass for the whole world to see. He stretched her arms out and made sure her legs were together, he then ripped her blouse opened, and buttons flew everywhere. He took the knife and carved just two letters into her sagging flesh of a stomach, the letters that showed not just Dalmuir, but the whole world that the ripper was alive and well and was continuing his work again.

He carved the letters that would haunt each and every person that knew about the crimes committed over the course of fourteen years. That knew the ripper personally.

The letters he carved were:

ZL

ACKNOWLEDGEMENTS

Thank you to my friends and family on yet again giving me ways to kill people – you are all sick in the head and I love it.

Thank you to my wife Rachael, for listening to my stories and giving me advice and what to do with the story.

And most importantly, thank you to my mum and dad for raising me the right way.

www.ingramcontent.com/pod-product-compliance
Lightning Source LLC
Chambersburg PA
CBHW071135310125
21189CB00025B/220